DOMITILLA AND THE GODDESS

ANTHONY HORNE

DOMITILLA
AND
THE GODDESS

Copyright © 2009 Anthony Horne

The moral right of the author has been asserted.

Apart from any fair dealing for the purposes of research or private study, or criticism or review, as permitted under the Copyright, Designs and Patents Act 1988, this publication may only be reproduced, stored or transmitted, in any form or by any means, with the prior permission in writing of the publishers, or in the case of reprographic reproduction in accordance with the terms of licences issued by the Copyright Licensing Agency. Enquiries concerning reproduction outside those terms should be sent to the publishers.

Matador
9 De Montfort Mews
Leicester LE1 7FW, UK
Tel: (+44) 116 255 9311 / 9312
Email: books@troubador.co.uk
Web: www.troubador.co.uk/matador

ISBN 978-1848760-400

British Library Cataloguing in Publication Data.
A catalogue record for this book is available from the British Library.

Typeset in 11.5pt Bembo by Troubador Publishing Ltd, Leicester, UK

Matador is an imprint of Troubador Publishing Ltd

Printed in Great Britain by the MPG Books Group, Bodmin and King's Lynn

AUTHOR'S NOTE

While the matter is not free from doubt, it is probable that when the Emperor pointed his thumb upwards at the conclusion of a gladiatorial contest this meant that the conquered gladiator should die by the sword. If the Emperor pointed his thumb downwards, this signified that the victor should drop his weapon and spare his opponent.

I wish to record my thanks to Pam Maplethorpe for her unfailing efforts in typing and correcting my manuscript, to Roger Staniforth for his helpful suggestions and amendments, and to David Morris for his design of the cover.

A.J.H

CHAPTER I

OSTIA

Near the docks of the port of Ostia a few miles down the river Tiber from Rome on the coast of Latium, there lived a woman called Alvia. She rented the rooms on the first floor of an apartment block between the Forum of the Corporations and the river. Alvia was not a very effective person; she was submissive and perhaps a little lazy. She had started life doing bar work in one of the taverns that were scattered about the area immediately behind the wharves where the ships docked. It was easy going, even if the wages were hardly enough to pay the rent. Men came and went regularly, coming in for a snack or a drink before returning to the task of unloading the grain into the big warehouses nearby. Alvia served the wine, kept in clay jugs under the counter for coolness, and washed the wooden platters and pots when there were no customers. The owner of the bar and his wife cooked the food on the gridiron heated with charcoal housed in the counter fronting onto the street.

One evening Alvia got rather tipsy with a sailor who plied her with several cups of wine. She had met him before as he did a regular run on a grain ship from Sicily and came in about once every two months. Alvia took little care of her appearance or clothes which rarely saw the inside of a fuller's shop or even the water from one of the public fountains.

However, she was not unattractive, with a neat figure and a pretty face framed by long black hair which was usually uncombed. When the owner called time she found herself being guided out of the bar and when she turned down the alleyway leading to her rooms the sailor followed, asking if he might stay the night with her as he had nowhere else to go. He said he would pay, without specifying for what. Partly out of tiredness and partly out of the need for a little extra money, she agreed to let him in. The sailor was no trouble that night. He was too drunk and she left him to sleep it off in one room while she went to bed as usual in the other. But in the early morning he came to her – she was still half asleep and hardly realised he was beside her. Perhaps she was still a little intoxicated by the wine of the previous evening, for she offered no resistance to his attentions and when it was over she snuggled up to her sailor quite happily. Before he left he gave her some money, six sesterces, more than she earned in a week at the tavern, and asked if he could return for one more night. His ship sailed the following day.

And so began the gentle but sure decline of Alvia. For some months she kept up her work at the bar, but with less enthusiasm than before. The word got around the quays and wharves. The stevedores on the riverfront were always on the lookout for women who would offer sex for money and the town was full of sailors with no home and no wife to go to, waiting for a ship to sail. Alvia began to entertain regularly in her apartment. She earned a lot more, so eventually she gave up work at the tavern altogether. During the day she hung around the riverfront or walked down through the forum past the Capitol and the temple of Rome and Augustus, sometimes as far as the sandy beach at the end of the main street, beyond the city wall. By evening she was always back near the docks and warehouses where the men finished their work about sundown. She was placid, easy-going, friendly and cheerful. It never took her long to find somewhere comfortable to sit in the warm evening air, heated by the reflection off the high walls of the grain stores. She had her regulars who knew where to find her and who she knew would pay up properly. She began to take more trouble with her appearance, applying a little rouge to her cheeks, some eye shadow and tying her hair neatly with a ribbon in a chignon at the nape. After all, the men were entitled to expect something for the money they paid. She made sure the rent was up to date and was even able to afford some new clothes and some more elegant sandals. If a man made a noise when he came back to the apartment, it would be his last night. She didn't want the neighbours to be upset and the proprietor of the shop underneath, a baker, who sold her fresh bread each morning, had once complained when a drunk had fallen down the stairs in the early hours.

Alvia lived comfortably enough in this manner for a couple of years, until she discovered that she was pregnant. She was honest enough with herself to admit that she had no idea who the father was. It might have been one of at least ten different men. Realising that there would be a lengthy period when she would not be able to earn money as she had hitherto, she found a job near the Laurentine Gate in the southern part of the town, helping in a laundry. The laundry was on the ground floor of a small apartment block and her new employer rented to her two rooms on the upper floor. The arrangement suited Alvia well. She felt a need to escape from the dockland area now that she was expecting a child. She had been able to save a little money and, where she now lived, nobody knew about her past. The work was not too demanding, though she disliked the constant smell of urine and the ribald comments of the men as they pissed in the pots left outside the entrance, to provide the fuller with his cleaning agent.

In due course Alvia came to her term and, with the help of the knife sharpener's wife who lived next door, gave birth to a baby boy, Ixus. She found a wet nurse for him and carried on with the job. In the evenings she looked after Ixus as he played on the floor of their little room above the laundry. It was a happy enough existence; the child seemed healthy and vigorous; he was never ill. Sometimes they walked down to the beach and looked at the sea, watching the ships sailing into the mouth of the river or heading northwards to the new port built by the Emperor Claudius.

When he was eight years old Ixus asked who his father was. Alvia had been expecting the question and told him that he was a sailor who had drowned at sea. She had always said the same thing to the women who worked with her at the laundry, when they gossiped as they beat the clothes on the slabs and then hung them out to dry in the sun. Ixus played in the street with the other small boys. From the start he seemed bright and mixed easily with his friends. Alvia was pleased. She felt secure in her new surroundings.

A couple of years passed at the end of which the owner of the laundry, Festus, suddenly fell ill. A doctor came and said it was some disease from the east, brought in on the ships by sailors from Syria, Egypt or Judea. He prescribed various medications and told the patient to rest. Festus, however, did not respond and his condition grew steadily worse. He lay on his daybed sweating feverishly while his anxious wife sponged his face and body. Alvia did her best to help. She worked longer hours and prepared food for the fuller's children when his wife was too busy. Festus grew weaker till he could no longer rise from his bed. He began to cough up blood and stopped eating. A few days later he was dead and his widow decided to move away to live with her brother, a butcher in Rome. The laundry was closed. Alvia found herself without a job and with a hungry child to feed.

For a few days she wandered around, looking for work. This time she was not so lucky; there seemed to be nothing in that area of the town. She drifted back to the streets and bars by the riverfront. She found some casual work in a wine shop but it wasn't enough to pay the rent on the rooms over the old laundry. She rented a single room in a block near the small market and the fish vendors' stalls. There was plenty of activity here during the day and Ixus ran about happily enough, watching the busy life of the port with all its comings and goings. He became streetwise. He learnt how to steal dates or pastries off stalls when the proprietor was engaged with a customer. He ran errands, particularly for harbour officials who were always sending chits to and from the quayside to the offices of the shipowners in the Forum of Corporations. He would go early in the morning and hang about near the temple of Ceres. Sooner or later somebody would shout, 'Boy!' from one of the offices behind the portico running round the square. Whoever got there first was given the errand and a small tip. Ixus became self-reliant. He kept himself fed and sometimes even brought back a little food for his mother. She never asked where it came from.

Occasionally, if there was no work to be had in Ostia itself, Ixus, with a few of the lads of his age, would hitch a lift over the river on one of the ferries. Then they would walk along the roadway across the Sacred Island up to the new port. As they approached they could see the great lighthouse, two hundred feet high, which stood on the outer mole of the harbour. It rose from a square base surmounted by two round towers, the upper one slightly narrower than the lower. At night a giant flame glowed from the lantern at the top. It seemed to Ixus, as he gazed up in wonder at it, that the flames would set light to the sky. Once, when they were unloading sacks of corn from a cargo boat into a barge on the canal which connected the harbour to the river, an old man told him that the mole on which the lighthouse stood was constructed from an enormous ship three hundred and forty feet long. The ship had belonged to an Emperor called Caligula. He had used it to bring an obelisk from Egypt to Rome. Later it had been filled with cement powder mixed with a compound which set like rock in sea water. Then they had sunk the boat to form part of the harbour wall. The man told Ixus about great buildings of gleaming marble in the city up the river from Ostia, including the enormous amphitheatre which had been finished some years previously. Ixus longed to see Rome and dreamed of it as he lugged sacks across the jetty from the boats to the barges, or lay on the mean little bed in the room which he shared with his mother.

Gradually Alvia slipped back into the life she had led before the birth of Ixus. She hung around the bars and markets, meeting the occasional man and taking him back to her room. Her looks had faded a little and she had to conduct her business during the day, as Ixus usually returned soon after sundown when there was no more work to be found. She began to drink more; sometimes she didn't bother to go out until the sixth hour or even later. Her head would feel thick from the excesses of the previous day. It took one or two cups of wine without any water added before she could face another day of sitting around, waiting for a customer, and then perhaps going out again. She had put on a bit of weight and her forearms were swollen with the squeezing and slapping of clothes at the fuller's. She lost the ribbon she used to tie her hair and didn't bother to replace it. On one occasion she never rose from her bed, but lay in the little dark room, taking occasional sips from a jug, slipping in and out of a sleepy torpor induced by the strong wine. Her face assumed an unhealthy pallor and her eyes lost the friendly sparkle of earlier times. In the space of a few months she changed from an attractive woman into something of a slattern. Instead of wanting to sleep with her, many of the stevedores laughed at this untidy slut who frequented the roughest part of the town. She could no longer pick and choose her customers but had to accept any man who was willing to pay. There were fewer and fewer of those.

Ixus was out and about all day. He rarely saw his mother until after dark. When he got home she was usually asleep and when she was awake, she seemed to have little to say for herself. Truth to tell, he found her company rather boring and he began to come home later and later, especially during the long evenings of summer. He had grown tall and strong, with a body bronzed by long hours of work in the sun. He found that he was attractive to the young girls who helped their parents in the little shops which lined the main street behind the theatre. They would meet to talk and flirt in the square near the baths of Neptune.

One evening in the early autumn Ixus said goodbye to his friends and walked back to the room near the fish market. He ran up the single flight of stairs as usual and opened the door from the landing. It was pitch dark inside, not even the little earthenware lamp burned in its usual place on the table in the corner. He reached up to the small window and opened the shutter. There was an unusual smell in the room. Slowly his eyes became accustomed to the shadowy light let in by the window. He made out his mother lying on the bed. At first he thought she was asleep but he could hear no breathing. He leaned over, feeling for her hand. It was so cold that he caught his breath. Her breast was damp and sticky.

Though he could not see it in the dark, Ixus knew that what he had felt was blood. His mother was dead.

He ran back down the stairs and stood for a moment in the alley, terrified by what he had found. He put his head in his hands and sank to the ground, shaking with fear and shock. There was nobody about. He must have sat for several minutes, rocking back and forth on his haunches, sobbing, opening and closing his fists. At last he stood up. He would go to the watchmen and report the matter. But when he reached their station house behind the public baths he could find nobody. The station was shut until the morning.

That night, which fortunately was warm and fine, Ixus spent sitting on a pile of timber near the waterfront. He could not return to the room where his mother lay. As soon as it was light he went back to the station house and found a watchman who came with him to inspect the scene of the crime. He was a kind man of some experience. Seeing Alvia's body he recognised her at once as one of the local prostitutes operating in his area. She had been stabbed in the chest, probably by a customer who couldn't or wouldn't pay. There was nothing to be done. The culprit would never be identified. It was not the first time he had been called to such an incident.

Ixus found a few sesterces in a leather purse hidden in the bedclothes. He knew a friend who had a cart. Together they wrapped his mother in the bedclothes and carried her down the stairs. They hid the body under a few sacks and wheeled the cart along the street through the forum and down to the Laurentine Gate, past the old fuller's shop where his mother and Ixus had been happy. They walked out along the sandy Via Severiana for a mile or two until they came to the little necropolis where the poor buried their dead. They made a pyre for the body out of some dry wood. It took a long time to burn. At last only a pile of ash remained with some bits of bone. These Ixus placed in an amphora which he had brought for the purpose and which he then buried in the earth up to its neck, where others had done the same. He worked mechanically until only the lead stopper was visible. His friend handed him a nail and he scratched, 'My mother, Alvia' in the soft metal. Then they wheeled the cart away and Ixus stopped crying.

The death of his mother changed Ixus's life very little. The landlord let him stay in the room. He could afford the rent and it was convenient for the waterfront. There was no reason to move. He took away his mother's bed, but otherwise his life and routine remained much the same. After the initial shock of her death he saw less of his friends for some weeks. He wandered about among the stevedores and sailors, staring into their faces and wondering if he was looking at the man who had killed his mother. He felt lonely and isolated. He lost his trust in people.

Yet Ixus was a resilient lad who had already learnt how to survive in a world where he had received little emotional or material support in the past. He was soon back at work on the docks, scouting round for unloading jobs or running errands for the customs officials.

A couple of months later the arrival of a ship from Africa caused a great stir on the quay. Ixus heard the roaring and trumpeting of strange animals and watched amazed as lions and elephants, which he had never seen before, were unloaded. He was told the animals were destined for the Emperor's menageries and ultimately the great amphitheatre in Rome. The elephants were to be taken to a park at Ardea while the lions would be held at Laurentum until they were needed. Barges came alongside and the elephants, hobbled with iron chains, were goaded aboard for transport by river.

The lions meanwhile roared angrily, pacing back and forth in their wooden cages which had wheels for easy manoeuvrability. Soon about a dozen large carts appeared, each drawn by a pair of stout white oxen. The drivers let down ramps and called for assistance to push the cages up into the carts, where they were lashed into position. Each driver had a mate who led the oxen on foot while his master kept an eye on things in the cart.

Ixus, fascinated by the animals, ran forward to help push a cage up one of the ramps. Each cage contained one lion and a cart could accommodate four. The driver issued directions while his mate helped with the loading. They soon had three cages in position. For the last one Ixus found himself pulling, while the driver's mate and another lad pushed from behind. Suddenly the driver's mate slipped and the cage rolled over his foot. He yelled out in pain, clutching his ankle. He had broken a bone and there was no possibility of his leading the oxen. Ixus saw his chance and asked if he might lead them instead. The driver looked him up and down, saw that Ixus was well built and asked if he had ever done it before. Ixus lied, saying that he had. Moments later he regretted it. The driver told him that there would be no pay for the work. The injured boy was a slave of the Emperor – Ixus would do it for nothing or not at all.

Once all the cages had been loaded the convoy started off through the town towards Laurentum which lay a few miles away to the south, along the coast. Ixus felt rather important for the first time in his life. The carts had an imperial escort of cavalry who cleared the way for them through the streets. The oxen seemed to be placid creatures, needing little or no guidance. He noticed that the other mates merely walked next to the head of the ox on the right, steering it occasionally with a gentle tap of their stick.

Beyond the city gate they followed the same road which led past the necropolis and his mother's grave. The quiet dignified progress of the oxen contrasted with the intermittent roaring of the lions. At one moment they were all silent, but the bellows of one would set off all the others until the air was filled with a continuous din. As they lumbered along Ixus saw the swamps and saltpans of the sandy terrain immediately to the south of Rome, while to his right lay the Tyrrhenian Sea. In a few hours they reached a hamlet called Vicus Augustanus and not long afterwards Laurentum came into view. It was almost dusk.

CHAPTER II

LAURENTUM

That night Ixus slept in a block with some of the other drivers' mates. They seemed friendly enough and gave him a little of their bread and salted meat. He realised that all of them were slaves. Round their necks they wore metal collars on which were stamped the words, 'Property of the Emperor Domitian'. They had not been born free like him, but he said nothing of this. It was assumed that he was a slave like the rest of them; after all, he had only one name.

In the morning Ixus found himself in an enormous compound where many different types of animal were held. As well as lions, he saw bears, tigers, seals, bulls, panthers, leopards and wild boar, all held in iron pens which stretched in long avenues radiating from an administrative block in the centre. In another part of the compound he saw hippos and crocodiles in concrete pools. One of the lads told him that enormous serpents lived in some pits at the end of one of the avenues. Ixus stood mesmerised but fascinated by the cacophony of roars, bellows and grunts which filled the air. The smell of excrement was overpowering. He watched men walking down the avenues, throwing chunks of meat into the pens. The big cats seized these greedily and the roaring gave way to the sound of crunching bones and growls. Down the centre of each avenue ran a stone channel with branches feeding water into sunken troughs inside each pen. The cats crouched on their bellies with their tongues lapping and their great eyes following the movements of their captors.

'These animals all belong to the Emperor,' said one of the other boys. 'They have to be kept well fed and watered; then they will fight bravely in the amphitheatre. They must be strong when the time comes for them to die'. Ixus walked a little further. He came to a cage with a human arm in it. In the next cage he recognised the leg of a man and a half eaten hand.

'These lions are fed on people so that they learn to like the taste of our flesh', said his companion. 'Criminals are sometimes condemned to be eaten by big cats in the amphitheatre. We have to train them for that', he said with a shrug. 'Often they bring back body parts from Rome in the carts, dead gladiators, the remains of criminals, whatever is left at the end of the shows'.

'How long do the animals stay here?' asked Ixus when they turned back.

'Depends what the Emperor wants. Sometimes there's a run on tigers and bulls. Then it's panthers and bears that are wanted. Of course, if it's a sea fight in the lake next to the Tiber they ask for crocodiles and hippos. There's stuff coming in and going out all the time. We'd better go. The drivers'll be shouting for us to go back soon'.

For the next few weeks Ixus worked as a driver's mate, making the daily journey to Ostia and back again in the evening. The driver, Sergius, was a free man who took a liking to his new assistant. He found Ixus good company and they became friends. Sergius spoke to the prefect of the menagerie, as a result of which Ixus began to receive a small wage. It was not long before he became a driver himself. He found he had a talent for handling animals. Not only oxen, but even the big cats responded to him. While other lions or panthers roared their protest as they bumped along the road to Laurentum, Ixus would linger at the quayside, talking to his animals before they set off. Very often he would have them lying quietly on the floor of their cage for the whole journey. There was no doubt that he had a way with these wild creatures. He felt comfortable in their presence and could imitate the different sounds of a lion, a leopard or a tiger with astounding accuracy. Men gathered round to listen to him. It was said that he talked to the animals as he walked down the avenues of pens and that the animals talked back. Ixus, still only a young lad from up the road at Ostia, became well known. Acilius Bassus, the prefect in charge of the menagerie, came to watch as he made a roaring lion, pacing round in his pen, stand still, then lie down and even purr at the sound of Ixus's gentle words. Others tried to imitate his methods but to no effect. The lions simply carried on growling and snarling. Acilius decided to keep Ixus permanently at the compound as one of the carers of the big cats.

The young man took an increasing interest and pleasure in his work. While he was not a loner, he found he spent more and more time around the pens. He tried to improve the conditions in which the animals lived, making sure the excrement was raked out of the cages each day. He had tree trunks placed inside and built platforms on which the cats could bask in the sun, with a shelter underneath. All the while he talked to them. They appeared to listen to his words or his imitations of their sounds. The other keepers called him 'the lion boy', though he had tigers, panthers and leopards in his charge as well.

Ixus began to settle into a routine. At the start of each day he and the other keepers reported to the office of the prefect's freedman where they would be informed of any deliveries of fresh animals from Ostia and of the requirements of the great amphitheatre and the gladiator schools in Rome. Ixus then prepared pens to receive the new consignment or selected animals to be carted away. The mobile cages were wheeled up to the hatches on the pens and secured by leather straps. With the hatches opened animals were lured by bits of meat into the cages. Ixus watched sadly as the carts lumbered away up the dusty road towards Rome. In most cases the cats never came back for they were slaughtered in the arena, unless men or women were themselves thrown to the beasts to be devoured by them. These animals, which had acquired the taste for human flesh, sometimes returned to be held in readiness for the next games.

The throughput was so great that Ixus had little time to get to know his animals or to develop any lasting affection for them. Indeed, he consciously tried to look upon them as items of stock to be received or consigned. Nevertheless, he could not help himself from doing his best to make them as comfortable as possible during their brief stay at the menagerie. Many of the animals arrived with sores on their bodies after the long journey from Africa or Asia in a cramped cage. Often they were close to starvation and had been given too little to drink in the transport ships. Ixus would talk to a lion with sores until it lay down on the sandy floor of the cage near the iron bars. Then he would clean the wound with a sponge on the end of a stick and apply unguent. He found that leopards needed no such treatment. The sores on their bodies soon disappeared because they licked themselves clean and the saliva quickly cleared up any infection.

Ixus spent the whole day by the pens where he had upwards of two hundred big cats to watch over. He rarely saw the other keepers at the menagerie, returning only in the evenings to the accommodation block. There he ate his food and was soon asleep once it was dark. It was not that he disliked his fellows, indeed he was friendly with many, but he felt more at ease in the company of animals than of people. He loved to stroll along the avenue during the long afternoons, watching the lions bask on their wooden platforms, or the leopards asleep on tree branches with their tails trailing in mid-air. He knew it was a brief respite on the long journey to a violent death in the bloody sand of the arena. There was nothing he could do about that. He would do what he could. He no longer wanted to go to Rome to see the great amphitheatre about which everybody talked in wonder. It represented the destruction of his work and care. He carried a long stick with which he occasionally tickled the neck or belly of a sleeping cat. Sometimes one would even nuzzle up against the bars of the cage, inviting him to tickle it. Then he would delight in listening to its contented grunts or purr, and try to imitate them. The lions and tigers purred spontaneously but the leopards were different. They would not allow themselves to be touched; instead he learned to imitate their purr and sometimes they answered with their own from their perch on a branch.

One morning a dozen or so carts parked outside the administration block where the clerks logged the arrival of the latest batch of animals from the port. Ixus knew that four African leopards were expected and had prepared pens accordingly. The cart with its cargo of cages came bumping down the avenue and Ixus supervised as the cats were each transferred to a pen. He noticed that a female leopard looked fatter and heavier than usual. After the cart driver and his mate had left, he looked again at his new arrivals. The leopardess had climbed onto a branch and was watching him balefully with her great green and yellow eyes. She had a tail as long as her body, covered with dark rings and a black tip.

She swished it angrily and occasionally gave vent to a noise which was a mixture of a growl and a bark. She looked a little uncomfortable with her fat tummy bulging over the sides of the branch. Ixus realised that she was pregnant. He had never experienced one of his cats giving birth and for some minutes he gazed uncertainly at her, wondering what to do.

That night, long after the other keepers were asleep, Ixus lay awake, thinking about the leopardess. He wondered about the cubs she was carrying. He became so restless that at length he climbed out of his wooden bed and stole out of the dormitory. The door was bolted from the outside but it was a simple matter to undo one of the shutters and jump a few feet to the ground. The compound was fenced and guarded at each gate; nobody patrolled elsewhere. The sky was clear and there was enough moonlight to see the sumptuous villas silhouetted against the skyline a mile or so away on the coast, where rich Romans relaxed, away from the smells and noise of the city. Ixus looked down into the dark pits occupied by bears brought from Asia. He could see nothing but heard the occasional grunt as an animal stirred in its sleep. He came to a high fence beyond which a giraffe was chewing some leaves. It started back in surprise and he heard its hooves padding in the sand as it hurried off into the shadows. He turned down the avenue lined with the pens of the big cats. Some lay asleep on the ground or had retreated into their shelters. Others silently paced round and round the perimeter of their prison. At Ixus's approach many stopped, crouched down and fixed him with eyes that glowed yellow in the faint light. It was as if he was walking along a path bordered by hundreds of giant glow-worms, each of which seemed to be focused unblinkingly upon him. A tiger was lapping water from its trough. As Ixus walked past, it looked up and then shook its great head to loosen the droplets from its whiskers.

A few hundred paces further on Ixus came to the pen he was looking for. The leopardess no longer lay on the branch which he had fitted about eight feet above the floor of the pen. Beside her on the ground he saw the remains of a wild pig of which she had eaten the hind quarters. Ixus could see the stains of blood on her muzzle. She had evidently been hungry but had made no attempt to drag the remains of the pig up into her 'tree'. He wondered if the cubs she was carrying made this too difficult, for he had noticed that most leopards stored their food off the ground.

Ixus squatted down to watch as the flanks of the leopardess rose and fell almost imperceptibly in the moonlight. She watched him intently. Even if she had been asleep, he knew that she would have heard him approach from far off. Presently she rose and climbed laboriously into the tree. She began to lick her paws and then to wash her face. Every now and then she paused to stare down at Ixus. He remained still and silent until at last her head came to rest on the branch and her eyes closed. Her tail ran like a snake back to the trunk of the tree. It ceased to twitch and even in his presence the leopardess fell asleep.

Some instinct prompted Ixus not to tell anybody of the condition of his new charge. The next day, when the cleaning, watering and feeding had been completed, he remembered an old set of pens which lay beyond the main avenue. They were behind a range of disused buildings which had once housed pigs and other animals for slaughter and feeding to the big cats. He decided to move the leopardess into one of these pens where she would be out of sight of other keepers and the prefect's clerks. It took him three days to construct a 'tree' behind which he built a rough shelter, consisting of old bricks, rocks and bars taken from other pens. Over the shelter he laid branches of pine to try to make it look more natural.

Ixus had to think and work quickly. He had no idea when the leopardess might give birth to her cubs. He realised it would not be long. She must have mated before leaving Africa and her belly was very swollen. He hung around the area where the carts and wheeled cages were kept. He found that he could pull an empty cage without too much difficulty, but wondered whether he could manage this by himself with a pregnant leopardess inside. If he were caught moving her without good reason, questions would be asked. He had seen slaves tied to a wooden frame and lashed to death with a leather thong for nothing more than stealing a bit of bread, let alone the property of the Emperor. But Ixus trusted nobody. He would have to do this by himself.

That night, as soon as both men and animals were quiet, he stole once more out of the accommodation block and fetched a cage. He wrapped the leather thongs used to pull the cage round his waist, like a harness. On the sandy soil the iron wheels turned almost noiselessly as he heaved his way down the avenue. From time to time he stopped to listen, poised to abandon the cage and flee back to the dormitory, if necessary. The eyes of the big cats watched him silently. He heard one scratching on a block of wood while another urinated against the railings. No human sound disturbed the night, for by now he was well away from the part of the compound where men lived. At length he reached the leopardess. He knew she would be alert and hungry for he had deliberately withheld her meat at feeding time. Now she was pacing up and down behind the bars. Her tail swished angrily and her plump tummy swayed as she padded ceaselessly from one side to the other. As Ixus fixed the cage to the pen she bared her fangs and hissed. She could see the lump of meat which he had secured inside the cage. It was the carcase of a dog whose legs Ixus had tied to the bars. He raised the hatch of the pen. At first the leopardess backed away, snarling. He held the hatch open at the end of a rope and stood away from it. For some minutes the leopardess crouched motionless on the sand. Ixus knew that she could see and smell the carcase; she would come for it. Suddenly she stiffened and with her tummy almost brushing the ground darted into the cage, where she began to lick the flanks of the dead dog. Ixus let the hatch drop. The leopardess spun round in a flash of gold and black, but it was too late. She snarled and hissed as he hauled the cage along the path beside the water channel. She was heavier than he expected. The ground sloped a little downhill; otherwise he could not have made the journey to the new pen. He had to stop and rest frequently. Each time he spoke to the leopardess. To begin with he made no impression but at length she stopped snarling and turned her attention to the dog. He heard the crunch of bone as she began to eat.

At last he reached the disused pen and secured the cage to its open hatch. Then with a knife he severed the ropes which held the dog carcase. He sat back to rest on his haunches, breathing heavily. The leopardess walked into the pen and began to sniff at the tree and the rough shelter. She padded slowly round the perimeter, spraying her scent against the bars. Ixus moved away from the cage, hoping that she would come back for the carcase. Eventually she came for it, lifting it in her jaws but making no attempt to climb the tree. The water trough had been filled earlier. Ixus knew that it would have to be checked every day, for the disused pens lay beyond the irrigation system. He hid the wheeled cage in one of the derelict buildings. He was too tired to push it back to the storage area and besides he sensed the approach of dawn. He had to hurry back.

For the next ten days Ixus watched and waited. Each afternoon he visited the leopardess, when the compound was quiet while both men and animals dozed in the sun. He had filled her old pen when a delivery of leopards had arrived from Asia. He noticed their colouring was different from the African leopards, with a cloudy grey background to the dark spots. He found them especially beautiful and dreaded the day when he would have to part with them. But his leopardess was the animal he really loved. He sat by her pen and waited for her to become used to his presence. Gradually her natural hostility diminished as she became accustomed to him. She ceased to snarl and hiss. Together they lay in the sun, she on one side of the bars, he on the other. Ixus wondered if he had been mistaken. Perhaps she was not pregnant after all.

One afternoon, when he came to the pen as usual, he could see no sign of the leopardess. He realised that she must be inside the shelter although he could not see beyond the entrance. He left food and filled the water trough. When he came back in the evening, after feeding time, he saw fresh droppings in the sand and the meat had disappeared. There was still no sign of Raca, the name he had given to her. He called softly, imitating her cough; there was no response.

For three days Raca did not appear. Ixus knew that she was alive and well for her food kept disappearing and he found her padmarks in the damp sand by the water trough. He became excited and impatient. Surely she had given birth; there must be cubs in the shelter. When would she bring them out to show him? On the fourth day at dusk he suddenly detected Raca's face staring at him from inside the shelter. He called to her and placed the body of a calf just inside the pen. He sensed that she was watching him while he filled the water trough.

It was another two weeks before Raca emerged. Ixus found her lying in the shade of the tree with a solitary cub suckling. He felt a twinge of disappointment. He had expected there to be more than one cub. The tiny creature bore no resemblance to her mother's colouring. She was a small bundle of dark woolly fur with no trace of spots. At the approach of Ixus Raca rose and slowly stalked back into the shelter. The cub, barely the size of a rabbit, followed, stumbling and falling over once.

During the months that followed, Ixus delighted in watching the cub's antics. She grew more confident every day, jumping up at her mother's tail and trying to catch the black tip in her paws. She splashed in the water trough and attempted to climb onto the top of the shelter, repeatedly falling off, only to start again. Within a month she had doubled in size and had started to chew at the hunks of meat or carcases left for Raca. One day Ixus found both of them on the branch of the tree, fast asleep. He sat down to watch. He experienced a great surge of affection for the sheer beauty and serenity of the animals in front of him. He could not imagine anybody wanting to harm them, let alone slaughter them in an arena before a baying mob of humans. He tried to stop himself from crying, but the tears came uncontrollably. Sooner or later Raca would go the way of every animal in the menagerie. She was logged and registered by the clerks. He would have to account for the property of the Emperor. He could postpone her departure as long as there were substitutes to take her place, but eventually she must go with the rest. Ixus had devoted all his care and love to Raca; nothing else mattered to him. His fellow human beings would subject her to a prolonged and agonising death. As he walked back through the compound Ixus watched some other keepers as they tossed food to the animals in their charge. They took no interest. Indeed they barely looked into the cages. Ixus did not hate them but he felt a sense of shame.

Summer faded into autumn. It began to grow colder. In the accommodation block Ixus heard talk about the feast of Saturnalia held at the winter solstice. The previous year all the animals in the menagerie had been cleared out and sent to Rome for spectacles provided by the Emperor. It was likely to be the same this year. Ixus lay on his bed wondering what to do. There could be no escape for Raca. He could not hide her indefinitely. But what of the cub? She did not exist in the books of the clerks. Perhaps he could at least save her from the arena.

By the calends of December when the prefect confirmed that every big cat in the menagerie was to be shipped to Rome for the Saturnalia, Ixus had devised a plan. He dug a small channel under the rim of Raca's cage, large enough for the cub to pass through but too small for the leopardess. He tied the leg of a sheep to a cord and shoved it into the pen while Raca basked in the sun. The cub, who loved to play, came to investigate. Gently he pulled the meat back towards him as the cub clamped her jaws on it. She wriggled under the bars and in a moment Ixus had the cub squirming in his arms. He carried her to the derelict buildings inside which he had prepared a temporary pen. Raca had not even woken. For a few days the cub would have to stay inside until they came for Raca. Then she could move back to her old home.

In the fading afternoon light Raca stood motionless in the middle of her pen. Every now and then she lifted her head and emitted a sound like a cough. She was calling for her cub. Her head went slowly from side to side as she looked round, searching the shadows. She turned and walked slowly to the entrance of the shelter, stopped, and came back to where she had been. Again she raised her head and coughed. She circled round and round the pen, pausing to listen. Ixus wondered if she could hear an answering call from the cub in the building close by. At length she crouched down in the sand to lick the piece of meat which Ixus had brought for her. She would not eat. Ixus made himself watch the leopardess. She could not know that his suffering was almost as great as hers. He wanted to punish himself for the pain he was causing to this animal who was his friend and whom he loved. He started to walk to where the cub was hidden. He knew that if he went close enough he would hear her whimpering in the dark. He made himself walk further until he detected a faint mewing sound. Ixus stood there listening. For a moment he felt an almost irresistible impulse to fetch the cub and return her to her mother. He found himself clutching the bars of Raca's pen so that his knuckles turned white. He banged his head against the metal, sobbing uncontrollably. He wished he had never come to Laurentum. In the morning the carters would come. The clerks would require him to produce twenty-five leopards and sixty-nine lions – mere numbers to be checked off against a list. Convoy after convoy would trundle into the distance on the bumpy road to Rome, to be replaced in a few days by the next shipment from Africa. Ixus stumbled away up the avenue. That day a little iron entered his soul.

CHAPTER III

BRUNDISIUM

The family of Norbanus came originally from the town of Norba about fifty miles south east of Rome. His father, Arrius, however, had moved to find work in the busy port of Brundisium in Calabria, down in the heel of Italy. Here, by diligence and innate common sense, for he had no formal learning, Arrius prospered and eventually rose to the post of harbour master. Of his three children two died in infancy, probably the victims of disease brought in on the ships from the east. Norbanus, however, was a sturdy, well-built child who from his earliest days displayed intelligence and ruthless ambition. His father sent him to the local grammaticus who taught sometimes in his own house and sometimes in the shade of the portico of the temple of Fortune beside the forum. Occasionally he took his pupils out onto the harbour mole and talked to them about the ships and the places they had come from. Euristhenes had a deep knowledge of Greek and Latin literature and had studied rhetoric in Athens and Rhodes. It was the boy's good fortune to listen to a man of this calibre in such an out of the way place as Brundisium. Under the guidance of his teacher the pupil from the big house down by the port learned to speak and write good Latin and passable Greek. But it was the history of Rome's military campaigns and her generals which fascinated Norbanus. He devoured

Polybius and Titus Livius in particular. He relived the campaigns of conquest and the struggles against the rival tribes in Italy when Rome was young. He studied the wars against Carthage and loved to discuss the careers of Fabius Maximus, Marcellus, Scipio Africanus and the tactics of Hannibal. Later Euristhenes introduced him to Caesar's commentaries on the conquest of Gaul and the Civil War. Sometimes the old grammaticus would read from the poets: Ovid, Virgil and the lighter odes of Horace. Young Norbanus would show interest for a while but sooner or later the conversation would return to military matters and the strategy of Pompey the Great, Marius or some other general.

When he was seventeen and had grown into a strong young man who excelled at wrestling and throwing the javelin Norbanus told his father that he wished to go to Rome and enlist in a legion. He was barely of recruitment age but Arrius was wise enough to know that nothing would get in his son's way. He gave him twenty gold pieces and a robust mule for the journey.

Thus it was that one bright morning in early summer during the last year of the reign of the Emperor Nero, the aspiring legionary set off up the dusty white road running northwards along the coast of the Adriatic. In those days it was not much more than a cart track but Norbanus progressed steadily enough with his few belongings stowed on the mule. To begin with he met farmers and sheep drovers from time to time, mostly bringing their produce into Brundisium to sell in the market. Gradually his encounters with other travellers became less frequent and he might walk for several hours without meeting anybody. At night he fed and tethered his mule, set up a small leather tent and slept soundly until first light woke him. He came to the village of Barium where the road turned inland and began to draw away from the coastal plain towards the mountains. Around him parched flatness expanded into the distance. Pits and trenches quartered the land to provide irrigation for vines and olive trees. Away to the west, flocks of sheep grazed on the greener lowlands. He had never seen so many sheep, for the terrain here was more suitable for pasture than the cultivation of crops.

One day he walked into the little town of Canusium past which the river Aufidus flowed down towards the sea. Norbanus remembered his lessons about the wars against Carthage. He knew that somewhere not far away the great battle of Cannae had been fought. He found an old man in the market place.

'You're a bit off track here, my lad. You see the river. Follow it down the hill. It's about ten miles. Keep on the right bank until you get to a tiny hamlet. That's Cannae. Hardly anybody lives there now. That's where it happened. That's where Hannibal killed fifty thousand Romans in a day. Up here the townswomen still say "Hannibal's coming" to their children when they misbehave. Most of 'em don't know what it means.'

Norbanus followed the river as it meandered down the hill into the plain. At length he found the hamlet perched on a tiny rise above a wide expanse of flat land which seemed deserted and uncultivated. He spoke to a man who was sitting on the threshold of a small round house with a pointed roof. He had never heard of any battle and Norbanus could find nobody else about except a couple of small children who were trying to trap rabbits. He walked down the slope and wandered around looking for some clue which would confirm the site of the battle almost three hundred years earlier. For some time he drifted aimlessly, tugging at the mule which kept stopping to graze on anything edible in the arid soil. Eventually he sat down to eat a piece of bread, irritated by his failure to find anything. As he did so he felt a sharp pain in his bottom. There was something in the soil beneath him. He pulled his dagger from his belt and after a little digging found himself looking at a fragment of a Roman legionary's helmet. His gaze wandered over the silent expanse of grassland in front of him.

In his mind's eye he sees the legions of Paullus and Varro drawn up in close formation, too tightly to manoeuvre properly, flanked by Roman cavalry on the right and allied contingents on the left. Opposite, a few hundred yards away to his right, the lightly armed skirmishers of Hannibal's army screen his Spaniards and Gauls drawn up in a crescent formation with heavy Libyan infantry concealed on each flank. On Hannibal's right are ranged the formidable Numidians, their brown faces and coloured pennants shining in the sun while their ponies paw the ground, waiting for the signal to charge the allied cavalry. On the left flank the Carthaginian general Hasdrubal marshalls his Celts to ride along the river bank into the waiting Roman horse. Hannibal himself, single eyed, watches and takes note. He knows that the confident Romans will advance into his soft centre – that is what he wants them to do. As the legions march forward with their battle trumpets blaring Hannibal gives the order to engage the enemy. His skirmishers run back through the Spanish and Gallic infantry which gradually give ground to the heavy legions, sucking them further and further into the trap. With a triumphant shout the Carthaginian swings round in his saddle telling his gallopers to give the order for the Libyans to turn inwards upon the exposed flanks of the advancing legionaries. His cavalry, having chased the Roman horse from the field, wheel about to take the legions in the rear. The jaws have snapped shut and the slaughter begins.

Norbanus stamped his foot and gave the mule a sharp rap on its rump. They set off up the hill to retrace their steps and continue the journey to Beneventum, high up in the rolling hills and mountains to the west. How near Varro had come that day to encompassing the ruin of the Roman state. The incompetence made him angry.

Past Canusium, following the valley of the Aufidus as it snaked into the hills, Norbanus and his mule walked upwards. He liked the evenings best when the sun cast long shadows over the summer pastures covered in sheep. Occasionally they met a drover with his cart and perhaps a dog but otherwise there was little sign of human life. When the sun sank behind jagged limestone outcrops high above him Norbanus welcomed the cooling shadows. Gradually the stones beneath his feet lost the heat of the day and often a light breeze sprang up. One afternoon near Trivicum the stony road along which they had been travelling, often interrupted by watercourses and sometimes washed away completely by winter torrents, joined the Via Appia. Norbanus marvelled at the smoothness of the paving, shaped at each corner and levelled to form a surface which appeared unbroken. His mule picked up a little speed, encouraged by the easier going. Norbanus noticed that each mile was marked by a stone indicating the distance to the next town. They came to Beneventum in the heart of the old territory of the Samnite tribe. Norbanus recalled the story of the Caudine Forks when a Roman army had been trapped in a gorge, disarmed by the Samnites and forced to bend double before walking under a yoke as a sign of defeat and humiliation. He felt his face flush with indignation.

Near the forum his eye was caught by the temple to the goddess Isis. At the top of the steps two giant crocodiles guarded the doors. Inside a statue of the bull Apis, carved out of porphyry and whose eyes were set with rubies, rose on a plinth of basalt above the smoky braziers.

After Beneventum the going became gentler, for now Norbanus was heading downhill towards Capua and the Campanian plain. He passed the city's amphitheatre, the biggest in all Italy then, and stopped to watch a public display of gladiators training at one of the schools. Each man carried a beam across his shoulders as he ran and jumped across an obstacle course, swerving in between wooden stakes to which spikes were attached, vaulting across ditches and balancing on a narrow swaying gangway. One mistake and the man felt the whip of the trainer on his bare torso before being sent back to start again.

At Terracina on the coast of the Tyrrhenian Sea the road climbed steeply to the sanctuary of Jupiter before falling away gently to the long straight stretching towards Rome. The highway grew busy with carts and carriages. Occasionally a squadron of cavalry clattered past and other travellers moved hastily aside to let them through. Inns and posting stations lined the road. Norbanus bought a new pair of sandals from a pedlar, for his others were quite worn through. The land lay lush and flat, full of crops and farmsteads where large white oxen drew the ploughs. He passed Velitrae and Albanum high up in the hills. On the last stage of his journey he glimpsed the giant arches of the aqueducts striding across the plain, bringing water from forty or fifty miles away to the thirsty citizens of Rome, their baths and fountains. On the twenty-seventh day after he had set out from Brundisium Norbanus stretched out his hand to touch the Golden Milestone set up by the Emperor Augustus at the end of the Forum.

★ ★ ★

Norbanus enlisted in the Legion VIII Augusta and saw several years of service on the Rhine frontier under the command of the legate Lappius Maximus. It was not long before he was promoted to the rank of rear spearman in the tenth cohort. By rigid attention to his duties and a natural aptitude for the disciplined life of a soldier he soon came to the notice of the tribunes and the prefect of the camp. It happened in this way. The legion was occupying a fort on the river at Neuss. Some time-expired legionaries who were serving an additional period in the reserve and were excused normal fatigues had been growing vegetables and keeping a few livestock on plots outside the fortifications. One of their number, a man in his fifties, had lit a bonfire and dozed off beside it. As night fell a raiding party of Germans, probably from the Sugambrian tribe, paddled across the river and began stealing vegetables and anything they could find from the plots. They discovered the sleeping veteran and, thinking he might be useful as a hostage, set off for the river with their captive and sacks of booty. Norbanus, who was on duty and had heard a disturbance, immediately ran in the direction of the river to investigate. In the half light he spotted a raft tied up to the bank and recognised it as the sort used by the Sugambrians. He concealed himself close to the bank among some reeds. Sure enough, within a few minutes three ruffians appeared carrying sacks. Two of them held the veteran whose arms were tied behind his back. When the third scrambled down the bank to untie the raft Norbanus sprang out and cut him down with his shortsword. Seeing this, the veteran lashed out with his legs and his two captors fled into the darkness rather than face the onslaught of the legionary who was running up the bank after them. For this actionNorbanus received a bronze medallion to attach to his breastplate.

Norbanus rose rapidly through the centurionate to the first rank of the first cohort and by the age of thirty-three he had been promoted to first spearman of the legion, the youngest first spearman in the army of Lower Germany. The post automatically elevated him to the order of knights and at the end of the year he was transferred to Rome as a tribune of the Urban Cohort, followed a few months later by appointment to a tribunate in the Praetorian Guard where the death of the tribune of the seventh cohort had created a vacancy. On parade he sported the ornate plumed helmet and oval shield of a guard instead of the rectangular shield of the legionary, but he kept his old breastplate embossed with a bull, the symbol of VIII Augusta which had been formed originally by Caesar in Gaul and seen action at Pharsalus, Thapsus and Mutina.

After service in Lower Germany Norbanus found the rankers of the Praetorian Guard soft and dissolute. He was gratified to discover that the vast majority were Italians, for his legion in the province had been composed mostly of local men who had never been near Italy in their lives. But these guards saw little active service abroad and spent too much time in the taverns of the city. Some even had bellies which protruded over their sword belts. Under the command of Norbanus, however, the men of the seventh cohort soon assumed a different appearance. He took them on route marches, gave them rigorous weapons training and insisted on immaculate uniforms. Their diet was regulated and any man found the worse for wine was subjected to a lashing and confinement to camp. Norbanus may not have been liked by his troops but he was certainly respected. The men would take private bets with each other to see who would be first to spot their tribune laughing or even smiling. Norbanus had few interests outside the army. All his energy was channelled into the efficiency of his cohort. He rarely dined with the other officers whose banter and chatter about the latest gossip in the city he found trivial.

All this was not lost on the Emperor. Domitian observed the difference between the seventh cohort and the rest of the Praetorians when it was the turn of Norbanus's men to guard the palace. Indeed he told the Prefect of the Guard that he would do well to raise the standards of the other cohorts to those of the seventh. It came as no surprise therefore that when a vacancy arose for the procuratorship of Rhaetia, where the Emperor had estates and other interests, he chose Norbanus to fill the post. It turned out to be a stroke of good fortune for the latter.

The governor of Upper Germany, one Saturninus, with an eye to seizing the empire and usurping the throne, decided to revolt not long after Norbanus had taken up his appointment. Saturninus raided the treasury of two legions, XIV Gemina and XXI Rapax before entering into an alliance with some German tribes to provide more troops and cavalry. He had reckoned, however, without the loyalty of Lappius Maximus who immediately marched against him with his legions from Lower Germany, having sent messages to his old subordinate, Norbanus, to advance northwards with his cohorts, thus trapping Saturninus in a pincer movement. Norbanus's troops, fit and well trained, had responded quickly to the threat, rendering valuable assistance in the rapid suppression of the revolt. The Emperor was again impressed. Four years later the youth who had set out from Brundisium twenty-five years previously took over as Prefect of the Praetorian Guard jointly with Tiberius Petronius Secundus. Norbanus had reached the highest post in the Empire available to a member of the equestrian order.

CHAPTER IV

DOMUS AUGUSTANA

It is the calends of March in the fourteenth year of the reign of Domitianus Caesar Augustus Germanicus, Emperor of Rome. With the first hour of the day the sun strikes the gilded tiles of the temple of Jupiter on the Capitoline hill. Soon a beam of light reflected from the golden doors of the temple will radiate across the roofs of the basilicas and statues below in the Forum, still in shadow.

In the palace of the Flavians on the Palatine hill, Flavia Domitilla, granddaughter of the late Emperor Vespasian, niece of the late Emperor Titus and niece of the present Emperor Domitian, lies in bed. Somewhere below, in the sunken garden known as the stadium the birds are singing their dawn chorus. Domitilla stirs, throws back the covers and steps down from her raised bed onto the floor of polychrome marble. She ignores her felt slippers and walks across to the window where a slight breeze disturbs the silken curtain. She looks out over the Circus Maximus in the middle of which rises the giant obelisk brought back by Augustus from Heliopolis, out towards the Aventine and Caelian hills covered by a sea of houses. The sun has not yet lit this side of the palace and she turns back for her shawl. There is still a faint chill in the air.

Her maid, Orestilla, sleeps on in a corner of the room, but

Domitilla does not wake her. Instead she sits down at her dressing table. It is of gleaming white marble quarried from Mount Pentelicus near Athens, supported at each corner by gilded caryatids. Her mirror, backed with silver and bearing a portrait of Venus in relief, is a present from Julia Sabina, her cousin, who died of an abortion some years ago, victim of the incestuous lust of her uncle Domitian. Domitilla observes the lines of sleep on her cheeks. They will disappear and leave a skin which is still that of a young woman, pure and milky. Her eyes, too, do not betray their thirty-seven years. They are a subtle shade, simultaneously grey and blue. They sparkle still with life. She takes a stick from an ivory box with a carved pomegranate handle on the lid and gently polishes her teeth. The trace of a frown flits across her face; she has always thought her nose was not quite straight, the result of some boisterous horseplay when young. Now she applies a touch of blacking to her eyebrows. Nothing more is needed to complete her toilet, for Flavia Domitilla has a naturally beautiful face which needs no further artificial aids. Her dark hair runs over her head in gentle silky waves, apart from two ringlets by her ears, a concession to the fashion of the times. Not for her the metal frame which supports the elaborate layered creations of the Empress Domitia Longina and other ladies of the court. She rises from the table and lets her tunic slip to the floor. Her slim body stands revealed. She is shorter than most Flavian women, perhaps a little over five feet tall, but her breasts are firm and her figure remains perfect despite the birth of children. She wears a necklace of tiny golden oak leaves from which hangs an aureus depicting her beloved uncle Titus. When Domitian first saw it he was jealous and demanded that she remove the coin. But Domitilla showed him the reverse, a representation of her two uncles shaking hands under the blessing of Augustan Piety, and the Emperor relented.

Orestilla hurries over to pick up the discarded clothes and lay out fresh ones in celebration of Matrons' Day. 'Has my lady remembered,' she asks, 'that today the court is moving to Albanun for the festival of the Quinquatria later this month?'

Domitilla has not forgotten. Recently she has sometimes found it difficult to fill her days. It will be a relief to exchange the tedium of Rome for the fresh air, the lake, the woods and hills around the Alban Citadel. Her husband, Flavius Clemens, has been appointed an ordinary consul for the first months of the year, jointly with the Emperor. His duties are largely ceremonial, for real power resides with the Emperor himself, his freedmen and his 'friends'. Nevertheless, Clemens will have to remain in Rome to preside over the Senate, if one can dignify with that title such a body of sycophants. A little uncomfortably Domitilla realises that she will not miss her husband in the country. Over the years Clemens has grown idle and inert. He does little but play at dice, attend the Circus to bet on the races or go to the amphitheatre to watch the gladiators and wild beasts. Each evening he drinks too much wine and falls asleep on his couch, waking late the following day to resume his tedious routine of gambling and spectating at the games. Domitilla flushes at the thought of his dissolute behaviour. The virile young man by whom she bore her children has turned into an obese and drunken oaf. It is yet another insult to the Senate that the Emperor has appointed him to the consulship, if only for the first part of the year.

She does not even have her sons, young Vespasianus and Domitianus, to look after any more. They have finished their studies under their tutor Quintilian and been sent to Trajan in Upper Germany to learn the art of soldiery. Thank the gods, they should be safe there. Domitian has nominated the boys to be his heirs, for he has no sons of his own. Domitilla has written to the governor, imploring him to keep her sons under his wing for as long as possible. To be too close to the throne is a dangerous place in the court of Domitian.

★ ★ ★

Inside the deepest recesses of the private palace, accessible by only one staircase and behind locked doors, the Emperor of Rome, ruler of the world from the Pillars of Hercules in the west to the waters of the Euxine lapping the tip of Armenia in the east, commander of twenty-eight legions and many more auxiliaries and allies, lies fretting on his couch. He has slept only fitfully. In his left hand he holds the commentaries of Tiberius on his military campaigns; in his right, a stylus which twists nervously in his fingers. The room is dim and airless, lit only by two narrow archways. Nearby, on a table, rests a marble bust of the Emperor himself and on its head sits his wig of tight brown curls. Irritably he claps it on his own bald pate. He flips the rolls of papyrus but does not read them. He cannot concentrate; his mind is restless. He feels under the pillows of his couch for the dagger which is kept there. Reassured, he rises and summons his valet Parthenius, the only person permitted to be inside the private apartment when he sleeps.

Parthenius, immaculate in the livery of an imperial attendant, a white tunic trimmed with gold, enters, bowing as he does so. 'Good day, my lord and god'. Before him he sees a man in his forty-third year, his wig askew above a ruddy-complexioned face, his legs spindly beneath his nightshirt which betrays a slight paunch. On the Emperor's chest hangs a little shield of goatskin attached by a leather thong around his neck. It is the aegis of his protective goddess, Minerva. This morning it twitches with the nervous movements of his larynx. On the other side of the room stands a statue of the same goddess in Corinthian bronze with ruby eyes and draped in a garland of laurel.

'Is everything prepared for the journey to Albanun, Parthenius?'

'My lord and god, it is. But a courier has arrived from Pompeius Longinus, your governor in Upper Moesia. He wishes to report on the strengthening of the fortifications along the banks of the Danube and the war against the Sarmatians. Do you wish to see him, sir?'

'No, no. He will have to wait. In fact, Parthenius, tell him to accompany us to Albanun and I will see him there. Before we leave I wish to talk to Crispinus. I will see him in the Sicilia after breakfast. Where is Euphemus? Tell him to bring some figs, some barley-cake and sausage. And tell him I want them tasted in my presence'.

In the shady porticoes of the Sicilia peristyle, hidden from the world, the Emperor takes his exercise, keeping his own company. The colonnade is lined with moonstone, so polished that a man can see his own reflection in it and observe anybody who approaches from behind. Here today the Emperor walks with Crispinus, one of his 'friends'. A German guard stands at each corner, watching outwards to the entrance doors.

'I have had bad dreams, Crispinus,' the Emperor mutters. 'I saw that the temple which I built on the Quirinal to honour the site of my father's house had been struck by lightning and destroyed.' His hand is shaking and he pushes it into the belt of his tunic to steady it. 'You realise what this portends, don't you?'

'My lord and god', laughs Crispinus, 'we all have dreams, some good and some bad. A dream does not necessarily predict the future. Your temple still stands, does it not?'

'I sent a slave at first light this morning to fetch the chief priest. He has reported to me that the temple is untouched'.

'Well then, last night you must have eaten something which disagreed with you. You probably didn't have the dream at all but awoke thinking you had'.

'Believe me, Crispinus, I had the dream for certain. There is evil in the air; I sense it. The gods have decreed that the dynasty of the Flavians is to be brought to a violent end'. The Emperor glances behind him though he knows that nobody is there. He tugs his companion's arm and pulls him down to sit by the fountain.

'Listen,' he says. 'I believe there may be more conspirators plotting to do away with me, supporters of the senators whom I have already been obliged to execute for their treasonable activities. What do you know?'

'My lord and god, I've heard nothing. But of course there's much resentment at the executions last year. Herennius, Helvidius and Arulenus all had their friends. People are asking who will be next. And then again there are those whose estates have been confiscated to defray the cost of your new buildings and the increased pay for the legions.'

The Emperor's mouth sets firmly. 'I must have money for these projects. "Let them hate me, so long as they fear me." That's what Caligula always quoted from Accius. If senators or any others breathe treason against me I shall not hesitate to strike them down. I have in mind, you know, to execute one or two men close to the household. It would set a good example to the rest.' His hand comes down sharply on a fly which has settled on the bench beside him. 'I shall squash them all like that. Then we'll see who is the master. Meanwhile, Crispinus, get our informers to work: Messallinus, Sura, Carus and the rest. I want results.'

'Of course, my lord and god. I take it that anybody is fair game if results are what is wanted.'

'One or two executions of ambitious men would help to keep the rest well cowed. We have got rid of the philosophy gang and some of the dangerous republican thinkers, but they must be kept down, like weeds. Find the evidence or, if necessary, manufacture it. I think we understand each other'. The Emperor turned and smiled thinly. 'You know, we emperors are unhappy men. Nobody believes in the existence of conspiracies until the dagger slides into our guts.'

Later, Domitian dismissed his servants and retired again to his room. He prayed to Minerva that she would continue to protect him. The words tumbled from his mouth in a muddled stream of pleas as he knelt before the statue, stroking its smooth metal with agitated fingers. He pricked his arm with his stylus and squeezed. 'If Flavian blood is to be spilt, please let that be sufficient to appease the Fates'. He gave a little grunt and grinned at his clever gesture. The ruby eyes of the goddess stared unseeingly back at him; he knew she understood.

At the sixth hour a line of carriages left the palace on the Palatine. On the slope leading down to the arch of Titus the way was lined with senators in their formal togas with the broad purple stripe. They bowed as the Emperor went past, then raised their right arms in salute, calling out, 'Hail to our lord and god, Domitian. May you reign for ever'. The procession, escorted by a detachment of the Praetorian Guard and some German cavalry, moved out past the great amphitheatre and its fountain onto the Via Triumphalis before turning into the Via Appia. In a few miles it would reach Albanum, the palatial retreat in the hills south of Rome, designed for the Emperor by Rabirius.

At Rome shortly before dawn on the following day an

elderly man stumbled out of the sleeping quarters of the imperial clerks and attendants in the private palace. In the dark on the gravel outside the library of Apollo they held him still. There was a single shriek as the needle smeared with poison pierced his armpit. He slumped forward and they dragged his body into the library. They placed it in a chair before some scrolls and a writing tablet. In the morning the librarians found him there. Poor Epaphroditus, recently recalled from exile and sometime Nero's secretary who had helped him to commit suicide, had died of a seizure, so they said. But Stephanus, Domitilla's freedman and steward, had heard the running footsteps in the night and seen the hooded figures. He said nothing. Others had been woken by the pleas for mercy echoing down the passages. Freedmen and slaves alike carried on as usual. On the Palatine hill it was safer to know nothing and to say nothing. You never knew to whom you might be talking.

CHAPTER V

ALBANUM

Domitilla walked along the underground passage from her rooms in the palace towards the peristyle where dinner was to be served. Some light penetrated from the windows high up in the vaulted roof but it was already dark and her servant Achilleus carried a lantern. She hated that passage. It was never more than dimly lit and was over three hundred paces long. Once, she had seen two praetorian guards standing outside a set of the large doors of studded bronze which lined the passage at intervals. As she passed she had heard a long drawn-out scream coming from inside.

Emerging into the peristyle she saw the Empress, Domitia Longina with her attendants. She looked anxious and upset.

'He's in one of his mad cruel moods. We're in for an unpleasant evening. Look over there.' Domitilla saw that the basin in the centre of the peristyle had been converted into a shallow pool. Where the fountain had been rose an island of jumbled rocks upon which a gilded throne had been placed. On one side in a cage lay three crocodiles on a flat slab sloping down into the pool. A lamplighter was moving through the porticoes of fluted columns which surrounded the courtyard, lighting brands of tallow whose smokey glow reflected in the water. In another corner of the pool were moored six wooden boats each of which contained an elderly senator. She recognised poor old Fabius Mauricus with his withered arm and Lucius Priscus who was over seventy, if he was a day. The Empress mentioned the names of two of the others. Domitilla was too horrified to listen. Each man sat hunched in his boat clutching what looked like a fishing line and enveloped in his toga.

Courtiers gradually arrived to take their places on the couches which had been arranged around the pool. Acilius Aviola, curator of the aqueducts in Rome, hobbled in. Domitilla had been relieved to see that he was not in one of the boats. He stood, propped on his crutch, talking to a group of imperial freedmen. Veiento was among them with his wife, Attica, who looked pale and nervous. A stick came tapping on the marble pavement. In walked blind Messallinus, the most hated informer of them all. He might not be able to see but men swore that he could hear a whisper at twenty paces. He leered a 'thank you' as he was guided to his couch by the obsequious Crispus. In the background, surveying the scene without expression, stood Norbanus, the Prefect of the Guard in his military uniform. As usual, the equestrians and the freedmen occupied the best seats while the senators had been relegated to the back.

'What hideous spectacle do you think he's devised for us tonight?' whispered Marciana, Trajan's sister, who had joined Domitilla on her couch. The peristyle was filling up. An imperial attendant climbed into a boat and pulled over to the island in the middle of the pool. He unloaded food and placed it on the ledges some feet above the water. The courtiers fell silent, trying to guess at the evening's entertainment for the Emperor.

Not far from where she reclined Domitilla noticed a tall fair-haired man standing by a pillar. He wore a fine green cloak held at the shoulder by a silver clasp. She had never seen him before and asked Marciana who he was.

'Oh, I'm surprised you don't recognise him, but then you've never been one for the amphitheatre. That's Hermes, the heart-throb gladiator of a few years back. You must remember.'

Domitilla did recall the name but had never seen him fight. Her gaze lingered; he had a striking appearance. Suddenly he looked her way and she hurriedly lowered her eyes.

'What's he doing at Albanum?' she asked.

'I believe he runs the Emperor's troupe of gladiators here. He certainly doesn't fight any more – too old. His real name is Hispo. Hermes was just his fighting name. Still handsome, isn't he?'

Domitilla did not answer. Two trumpeters with large curved horns sounded a flourish. The double doors of the hall swung open and Domitian strode in wearing buskins and a purple cloak. On his wig he wore a simple band of gold entwined with a purple ribbon, its ends hanging loosely at the nape of his neck. By his side, grinning stupidly, waddled his eunuch, Earinus. He carried a bronze trident whose tines were tipped with gold. Everybody clapped. The pair were helped into a boat and paddled across to the island where the Emperor installed himself on the throne. Earinus handed him the trident and then squatted obscenely on a rock beside him. The Emperor raised his arm for silence.

'I've invited you all to dinner to mark the start of the festival.' He gazed round at the leaden faces of his court, of men and women who hardly dared to look but must not look away. 'But we have some special guests tonight, gentlemen who know and love me well. You'll forgive me if I feed them first.' He inclined his head towards the six senators in the boats who, as one, raised their right arms in salute and said, 'My lord and god, we thank you for your graciousness.' Poor Mauricus dropped his fishing line and had to scramble about in the bottom of his boat looking for it.

How the six senators were to dine soon became apparent. Using their hands they paddled out into the pool. With their fishing rods they reached out of their boats and tried to hook up the pieces of food laid out for them on the ledges of the rocks. Any senator showing a disinclination to take part was encouraged by the Emperor, insisting that he must eat like the rest. There was a stir among those sitting closest to the rim of the pool. A slave had come forward and raised the hatch of the cage housing the crocodiles. At first none of them moved. The slave prodded one with a spear. It reared up and stood for a few moments with its jaws agape before shutting them with a sudden snap that everybody heard. Slowly it waddled to the water's edge and slithered into the pool. Only its black eyes, snout and a small area of bark-like back broke the surface as it glided smoothly through the water. Moments later the pale belly of a second crocodile plumped into the basin. The third refused to move despite the prodding of the slave.

Domitilla felt Marciana's hand close tightly on her arm. The Emperor smiled and beckoned to a white-haired senator who paddled with his hand towards the island. The boat ran aground on the rocks a few feet short. Both crocodiles were on the far side and the old man stretched out with his line over the water, reaching for a stuffed pastry shaped like a turtle dove.

'Your life, dear Licinianus, is on the line. You must catch that bird or I cannot answer for your safety'. The Emperor's voice contained a hint of menace not lost upon the old man or those watching in dead silence. He stretched a little further, straining to hook the pastry. Part of his toga dropped into the water. Nobody saw the crocodile until it pounced, seizing the strip of cloth. It clamped its jaws on the toga, rearing up and thrashing the water with its tail as it sought to drag the poor man from his boat. Several women screamed and for a moment pandemonium broke out. The senator rolled over, somehow freeing himself of the toga which disappeared under the water with the crocodile.

'Bravo, bravo, Licinianus,' cried the Emperor waving his trident at him. Poor Licinianus paddled frantically to the rim of the pool where he and his companions were hauled from their boats. The crocodiles were fenced off with metal grilles before the Emperor left the island and departed with Earinus for his bedroom. People stood about in groups, speaking quietly, wondering what the next humiliation might be.

'They say that Caligula was terrifying and I saw Britannicus writhe in agony after Nero handed him a cup of wine,' said one old senator, 'but this monster is as cruel as both of them put together.'

'Not so loud, Quintus, your tongue will be the death of you,' muttered his companion.

'It's lasted me seventy-five years and I don't much mind what happens to me now. That man has done nothing but insult and bully the senatorial order since he came to the throne. Now he's become both mad and cruel just as the Claudians were.'

★ ★ ★

In the theatre, as part of the festival of the Quinquatria, the poetry competition was taking place. Statius was reciting an interminable poem praising the Emperor's achievements in the war against the Sarmatians on the Danube.

'I expect he'll win the golden olive-crown again,' Domitilla heard Julia Frontina say. 'He's won it twice before. He seems to be more skilful at flattering the Emperor than the others.'

The chief judge for the competition, Titinius Capito, was sitting next to the Emperor who clapped enthusiastically as Statius bowed and resumed his seat. The audience's eyes turned to Martial, the next competitor. Domitilla took the opportunity to slip away, telling her maid that she was going for a walk.

She climbed up through the woods behind the palace, stopping occasionally to smell the wild hyacinths which lined the path as it wound towards the ridge of the hill. Soon, high above the lake, she reached a clearing in the trees where a small round temple stood, topped by a tiled roof supported on six fluted columns. She sat down to rest on the steps and pondered idly why the temple should be there. Looking around, she noticed a shrine a few yards away by a bush of myrtle.

A shallow apse lined with blue mosaic sheltered an oval basin filled with the water from a spring which bubbled from the spout of a jug held in the left hand of a statue. In her other hand the figure carried a sistrum with a tiny she-cat inside. Domitilla recognised the goddess Isis. From her forehead rose the sacred asp. Her robe was saffron, tied under the breast with the mystic knot peculiar to the goddess.

As she gazed down at the marble figure whose unmoving face surveyed the lake below, Domitilla began to understand. Here flowed the waters of the Nile, flooded every year by the tears of the goddess, bringer of fertility to the land. In mourning the death of her husband her grief gave life to others. On the mosaic, papyrus boats plied up and down the wide river on the banks of which crocodiles basked and ibises roamed. Isis set off on her journey across the sea to the wells of Byblos in Phoenicia where she found Osiris, dismembered by her wicked brother, Seth. She beat her wings and breathed life into her dead husband/brother.

Restored to Egypt, Osiris now dwelt in the shady marshes of the Nile delta, king of the underworld, alive among the dead. Their son Horus entered upon his heritage, lord of the kingdoms of Egypt.

Domitilla knelt down by the statue. She felt the overflowing compassion and affection of the goddess and the protection which she brought to the young Horus while she nursed him back to health from his infant weakness. Isis was a goddess who descended to the people, who listened to the lonely pleadings of humanity. She did not look down haughtily from the golden temple of some lofty capitol, nor thunder like Jupiter from the summit of a distant mountain. This goddess was the sacred mother, the giver of life to all things, the protectress of the soul. She had the power to resurrect the dead, to alter destiny. On the pedestal Domitilla read the inscription. 'Even the Fates hearken unto me.' Her soul was uplifted by the simple goodness of the figure before her. She lost all consciousness of herself; her body became enfolded in the saffron robe. The murmuring of the spring and the scent of the hyacinths intoxicated her. A prayer came into her mind: 'O Isis, lead me. Release me from all things that are bad and evil and belong to Seth, from the tyranny that afflicts us, as you saved Osiris and nurtured Horus in the ways that are good.'

★ ★ ★

In the afternoon the Emperor was in the habit of practising his archery and Domitilla found it easy to slip away unnoticed to the shrine on the hill. She did not always pray to the goddess. Sometimes she simply sat on the steps of the temple, looking down over the lake and the sprawling palace on the slope above it. She preferred to be alone where nobody would intrude upon her relationship with the still figure standing on the rim of the basin. Her mind slipped into a reverie; she pondered on the mystic powers of Isis to heal and resurrect; and on Osiris, the kindly god of the underworld who listened to the souls of the departed and gave comfort, reassuring them that they would live again in the bodies of others. She pictured the boy Horus who had fought so bravely in the struggle with Seth to overcome evil. In the mosaic he lay in his mother's arms; in her mind Domitilla loved to hold him. On the hillside her loneliness dissolved in the company of the goddess. She found solace and comfort from the emptiness of her life at court and the loss of her own family.

One afternoon while she knelt at the shrine she felt a few drops of rain. She rose and moved inside the round temple for shelter. The rain soon eased and the sun emerged to glisten on the lake below. She heard the sound of footsteps crunching the pine needles in the wood behind her. A moment later a man appeared and she recognised Hispo whom Marciana had pointed out in the peristyle a few evenings previously. He walked swiftly and lightly over the ground with the easy movements of an athlete. He wore a tunic with a thick leather belt and knee-length boots. At his side hung a quiver of arrows and the bow was slung over one shoulder. Round his neck was draped a dead wild pig whose trotters he clasped with his hands. Domitilla watched as he dropped the carcase to the ground and knelt before the shrine. At first she thought he was going to pray but then he cupped his hands and drank. He threw a little water over his head and stood up, turning as he did so.

At the sight of Domitilla he inclined his head. 'I'm so sorry, my lady, I didn't see you there. Otherwise I wouldn't have…' His words trailed away.

'Please drink as much as you wish. The spring doesn't belong to me. You have been hunting, I see.'

'My lady, the Emperor is kind enough to let me roam these woods and take what I find.'

Domitilla stepped out from the temple and walked the few steps to the shrine. 'For a moment,' she said, 'I thought you were going to pray to the goddess. Do gladiators have any gods?'

Hispo stood in silence, contemplating the question. Domitilla observed the strong neck muscles as he ran his fingers through his pale hair to smooth it away from his face.

'I'm not sure that gladiators can have gods. When I was recruited I swore an oath to endure branding, chains, flogging and death by the sword. To die bravely was all that mattered. It didn't leave much room for the gods.'

'But you have survived. You have earned your freedom. Don't you feel gratitude for that?'

'My lady, I have watched as men that I have killed, sometimes my friends, were dragged with an iron hook from the arena. I survived because I was bigger, stronger, fitter and more skilled than they. Perhaps it was the gods who saved me or perhaps it was they who placed me in the arena. Why should I thank them for that?' He bent to pick up the wild pig and hoisted it upon his shoulders. Once more he inclined his head and apologised for disturbing her solitude. Domitilla watched as he strode away down the slope towards the gladiators' barracks on the far side of the palace. She watched him until he disappeared from view behind a fold in the hill.

★ ★ ★

Domitian ate a heavy dinner as usual. His eyes darted from one couch to the next. He was singling out a suitable partner for his 'bed-wrestling' as he liked to call it. The Empress had seen it all before – many times. She retired with her companions well before the end; it was less humiliating. Seeing this the Emperor beckoned to Dasumia Polla lying on a couch near to him. At first she pretended not to notice but soon she rose and walked unsteadily to where he reclined, propped up on an elbow with a pile of his favourite Matian apples at his side and a pitcher of wine. He patted her bottom and motioned to her to sit on the cushions next to him. The talk elsewhere became louder as everybody hastened to engage his neighbour in conversation. It would be dangerous to catch the Emperor's bloodshot eye. Now he had a flabby hand clasped around her waist and his head lay in her lap. Dasumia knew her duty, stroking his wig carefully so as not to dislodge it. At the back of the hall the imperial litter appeared and a few minutes later it was borne away through the revolving door, carrying the Emperor and his companion for the afternoon.

On her couch Domitilla relaxed. Marciana and Julia Frontina were discussing the latest fashions in the city and the affairs and scandals which occupied the minds of rich women who had little else to fill their time. Domitilla half listened to the chatter. Her thoughts turned to the shrine up on the hill, to the goddess who, she believed, protected her. Isis rose above the ceaseless daily round of feasting, drinking, sexual perversions, violent deaths and cruelty which invaded her own existence. Even the silver cup in her hand showing skeletons in a Bacchanalian orgy had engraved upon it the words, 'Enjoy life while you have it, for tomorrow is uncertain.' She remembered that on the eve of celebrating their triumph for the capture of Jerusalem her grandfather Vespasian and her uncle Titus had passed the night in contemplation of the goddess in her temple at Rome. She would go there too.

The other women were debating the question of who was the handsomest man in Rome. Domitilla looked up and saw Hispo standing with a group of young men on the far side of the hall. As she watched he turned and looked straight at her. She sensed he knew already where she was and dropped her gaze immediately. She beckoned Orestilla forward and they set off down the long passage beneath the lower terrace. She felt a slight palpitation in her breast and decided to lie down to rest on her bed of swansdown for the afternoon.

In the evening, as part of the festival, a play was being given in the theatre. It was a comedy by Terence called 'The Eunuch'. Domitilla, dressed in silk and muslin, arrived early and took her seat in the second row. The tallow candles flickered in their lanterns round the stage. Domitilla loved this part of the day; the soft light, the buzz of anticipation in the audience, the sparkling jewels in the hair of the ladies of the court, though she wore none in her own, and the shadows reflected on the wall behind the stage. She caught sight of Hispo walking across the space in front of her. He turned up the gangway by her seat and this time she did not lower her gaze. He paused, smiled and said something which she did not catch before climbing up the steps to a seat somewhere at the top. In the row behind Domitilla, Mummia Nigrina whispered in the ear of her husband. The Emperor arrived and moments later Latinus limped onto the stage, complaining that he had been forced to have his testicles removed to play the starring role of Chaerea, but that he would have them sewn back on immediately afterwards to comply with the Emperor's law forbidding castration. Even the Emperor laughed at that.

It was a beautiful morning when Domitilla stepped onto the terrace the following day. She turned left, instead of right.

She would try another route up the hillside to the shrine. She walked past the stables and under the arches of the aqueduct bringing water to the palace. The path snaked upwards into the woods above. She kept just inside the line of trees, above the grassy slopes where she might be spotted from below. She climbed steadily and then sat down to rest by a clump of wild violets. Below, the palace complex stretched out in a panorama. Domitian was practising his archery. She could just make out the figure of a tightrope walker poised above a pit while the Emperor fired his arrows, trying to knock him off. A little further away beyond the circus she saw the square of the gladiator barracks. In an oval arena beside it tiny figures darted, practising their skills with what looked like wooden swords and tridents. She thought she detected Hispo's blond head as he stood in the centre, occasionally gesticulating as he gave instructions. She watched for some time.

Eventually she rose and walked on through the woods, circling round until she reached the ridge of the hill above the palace. She found the path leading down to the little temple. As she emerged into the clearing a tremor ran through her body. A figure with his back to her stood by the shrine. She knew immediately it was Hispo. Instinctively she stepped back into the trees but he turned and saw her. He smiled and half raised his hand in greeting. From his belt hung two rabbits. Yet Domitilla sensed that he had been waiting for her. Had he seen her climb the hill and guessed where she was going? She came on down the slope.

'My lady, I must apologise again for intruding on your privacy. I have been out early this morning.' He paused. 'May I ask if you enjoyed the play last night?'

'I always enjoy Terence's comedies, though it was a bit bawdy. Latinus is very amusing, isn't he?' She walked over to the steps of the temple and sat down. He followed uncertainly and squatted on the ground with the rabbits splayed out beside him. Perhaps, she thought, he really has been hunting.

They began to talk. He told her how he had worked as a young man for one of the marble importers at Ostia. He had been employed to trim and face the great slabs which came into the workshops; yellow marble from Africa, pink from Chios and sea green tinged with blue from Euboea. But he had no talent for the work. His chisel often slipped and then his master would deduct money from his wages. He had humped bales on the docks to supplement his earnings, but that was a grim existence with no prospects.

'How did you escape from that life?'

'One day the owner of one of the gladiatorial troupes in Rome came down to do some recruiting. He had a couple of the big stars with him, Celadus and Thrax. They'd made a lot of money and been presented with prizes by the Emperor: jewels, horses and even houses, because of their success in the arena. I was young and strong, bigger than most. I knew I was quick and could fight. I always came out best in any brawl when I was a kid, and later in the taverns by the docks. I volunteered. Anything seemed better than the drudgery of that marble workshop.' He stopped. Domitilla prompted him.

'So what happened then?'

'They took me up to Rome, to the gladiator school called the Ludus Magnus, near the great amphitheatre. To begin with I was put in fetters so that I couldn't even stand up straight. Then the training started. Up at dawn to exercise, practice with wooden weapons. Later we went into a mock arena and trained with heavier weapons than the normal ones to build up our strength. I once stole some bread and was put in the prison block for a week; no food, only dirty water. Normally the food was good. We were given barley to supplement our diet and develop our muscles.'

'What sort of gladiator did you train to be?'

'I was lucky. My "doctor," that's the name we give to the instructors, was a retired Murmillo and he taught me to be the same. They're the Emperor's favourites. Not so good if you're a Thracian or a Samnite, especially a Thracian. He never seemed to like them.'

'How old were you when you had your first fight?'

'Me? About twenty-three, I think. I had to go to some funeral games at Capua. Poor bloke, it was his last fight before retirement. He was a bit slow and I got him quite quickly with a blow on his sword arm. He put his finger up to ask for mercy, but the magistrate in charge wasn't having any. I had to run him through.'

'How did you feel?'

Hispo shrugged. 'Well, I suppose it was him or me. Just like the other fights were. We were trained to die bravely. Sometimes I hoped I would, but when it came to the point I was always desperate to survive – instinct, I suppose.'

'Did you ever have to ask for mercy?'

'Once, in the great amphitheatre. A Samnite got me in the thigh. I was losing blood and couldn't move properly. We'd been fighting a long time. Eventually I went down and looked up at the Emperor. The crowd were all waving wildly with their thumbs down. I think they thought that I had fought well. Anyway the Emperor raised his handkerchief. I doubt he'd have done that if I hadn't been a Murmillo.'

'I seem to remember you had a pretty big following a few years ago. The people must have taken a liking to you.'

He looked up and smiled. The brown eyes and the firm line of his jaw pleased her. 'I had a good run. I won nine fights in three years. They seemed to like the way I fought. I even used to get mobbed in the street. Once a crowd of women tore the cloak off my back and then divided bits of it between them.'

'Yes, I can remember seeing the posters stuck up round the amphitheatre and in the streets; "Hermes fights here next week" in big red letters. That sort of thing. You were the crowd's hero.' Domitilla was conscious that she had spoken too enthusiastically. A little colour came to her cheeks.

'I was very lucky. In the end the Emperor gave me a million sesterces, my freedom and the use of some rooms in Nero's old Golden House. They're very close to the gladiator school. I always stay there when I'm in Rome.'

'Oh! I used to live there as a child. My grandfather knocked most of it down. Your rooms must be in the wing on the Esquiline that's still standing.'

'Right at the end, my lady. I think I'm the only person there now, apart from my slaves of course. They keep the place ready for me.'

Domitilla looked down at the man squatting before her. Even in that position he held himself proudly, with his broad shoulders squared to the world. 'You've come a long way, from a marble workshop in Ostia to an Emperor's palace.'

'Perhaps the gods ordained that for me.' He looked up and grinned. 'They always used to tell us to pray to Hercules – he's the god of gladiators. I never did.'

'So you told me.'

They sat in silence for a few minutes. Domitilla could not help herself. The desire for solitude in that place had left her. Eventually Hispo stood up, saying that he must get back to the barracks. He was training the Emperor's troupe in readiness for some games in Rome shortly after Domitian's return.

'Perhaps when I pass next time I shall pray to your

goddess. This is a place of peace and quiet. It would be nice to experience a little of that before I die.'

He strode off down the hill with the rabbits swinging at his hip. Domitilla knelt at the shrine and sipped some water. She tried to pray but could not concentrate.

★ ★ ★

In the centre of the oval arena stood a wooden pole with two crosspieces, one at knee and one at shoulder height. As the top piece revolved past him Hispo patted it with the palm of his hand to keep the pole spinning. The two tiro gladiators, wearing only short leather skirts but each carrying a wooden sword and shield, jumped and ducked as the crosspieces came around. Every now and then one was hit in the face or shin – Hispo merely increased the pace.

When the last pair had finished he noticed a lad leaning against the fence, watching the training. They didn't usually attract spectators; there were few who had time for that. The lad looked well built and had an air about him which attracted the older man. He walked across.

'Do you want to be a gladiator then?'

Ixus straightened up. He was nearly as tall as Hispo. 'No, sir. I was just watching out of interest.'

'Where do you come from, lad? I haven't noticed you around before.'

'I've come from Laurentum, sir. We're bringing animals to the Emperor's menagerie here. This is the first load. There's a lot more to come. Will they get killed in this arena?'

'No, no. This is just a training school. We don't kill anything here. These men are being taught to fight each other. They're going to be proper gladiators, not the lousy types who just slaughter beasts.'

'So why does the Emperor want all these animals from Laurentum?'

'Probably just for display. I think he likes the idea of having big animals around him. It gives him a sense of power.'

'Have you ever seen the Emperor, sir?'

'Yes, I see him frequently; every day when he's here.' Hispo laughed at the young man's surprise. 'You'll probably see him as well if you come here often enough. Have you never seen him in Rome?'

'I've never been to Rome, sir. I used to live in Ostia but I started working at Laurentum a few months ago.'

'Ostia, eh. I lived there as well until I was about twenty.'

Ixus was too young to remember any of the people, but he knew some of the bars and taverns which Hispo mentioned and he thought he could picture the marble workshops where Hispo had worked. They reminisced until Ixus had to go. He was glad he had persuaded the clerk to let him make the trip for a change. It had been exciting to meet a man who actually spoke to the Emperor. Over the next few days, as the carts came and went, Hispo saw young Ixus occasionally in the distance but never close enough to speak to. He always waved and Ixus waved back.

★ ★ ★

Domitilla hurried along the path and up towards the shrine. She made no excuses now but simply set off at about the sixth hour, leaving the other ladies of the court to gossip on the terrace. She loved the tranquillity of the little clearing with its view across the stillness of the lake.

She knelt down as usual by the statue and began to pray. She asked the goddess to protect her sons, so far away in

Germany. She tried to pray for her husband, Clemens, back in Rome discharging his duties as a Consul. It was her wifely duty, she told herself, to seek the goddess's protection for him. Yet, even as she mentioned the words, the image of Hispo came into her mind. In the days since their second meeting she had found it difficult to banish him from her thoughts. They had met often and, though neither acknowledged it, they both knew that their encounters were no longer by chance. Domitilla had fallen in love; it frightened her. She wrestled with her conscience. How could she pray to Isis, protectress of the family, and at the same time think of a man who was not her husband? She was a member of the imperial family. Did such people fall in love with a retired gladiator? She had often heard of patrician ladies taking gladiators as lovers; the daughter of a senator had actually eloped with one. She tried to dismiss these thoughts.

On the mosaic in front of her, the temple at Memphis rose beside the Nile and linen-robed priests bore down to the shore the ship in which Isis would sail in search of the body of Osiris. In her mind Domitilla heard the flutes playing and the antiphony of the choirs at each side of the procession. Like a priest about to sacrifice she draped her shawl over her head to shut out the rest of the world and concentrate upon the ritual in the picture.

Hispo came down into the clearing. She heard his footsteps crackling on the pine needles. She did not look up; she knew that it was him. Her heart beat faster and she could feel the thump in her breast resting against the basin. He knelt down beside her but did not speak. She had never been so close to him before. The pale hair glistened on his forearm. There was a livid mark on the back of his left index finger. She had seen him chew it from time to time. She put her hand on the statue to stop it shaking. Gently he placed his hand over hers. Still neither spoke. She gave a nervous laugh.

'You know if the Emperor saw you do that there would be serious trouble. He might do anything to you. And I am a married woman,' she added, and then bit her lip, regretting that she had said anything. Hispo rose to his feet.

'My lady, I am sorry if I have offended you. I had no right to be so familiar. I was forgetting my position.' He turned to walk away down the slope. Domitilla could not help herself. She called to him to come back.

'I didn't mean you to go; please stay if you would like to. Let's go and sit on the steps, like we usually do.' She took his hand.

The awkwardness between them had passed. The barrier of uncertainty had fallen away. The doubts had disappeared. They talked only of banalities; it did not matter. The fear and isolation of her recent life dissolved in the shadow of the temple. Domitilla felt her soul break free. She bathed in Hispo's smile.

As the sun dropped down towards the ridge and half the lake turned glaucous in the fading light he took her hand and led her inside the temple's little cell. He bent to kiss her on the forehead but she reached up and found his lips with hers. He felt her tremble as he closed his arms around her waist. She broke away.

'This is dangerous. I must get back and so must you, before it gets too dark'. She pulled his face down to hers once more and then hurried down the steps away into the evening air. Hispo waited for a few minutes, watching her recede into the distance. She did not turn to wave. Then he set off up towards the ridge, striding quickly, watched by a pair of eyes behind the trees.

Three days later a line of carriages left Albanun, rolling steadily northwards up the Via Appia towards Rome. Hispo told Domitilla that he would send a message when he returned to the city.

CHAPTER VI

ROME

In a house on the Quirinal hill four men were playing at dice. The house belonged to Flavius Clemens, Domitilla's estranged husband. The men with whom he was playing were the charioteers: Scorpus, Polemus and Minicius. It was head to head now between Flavius and Scorpus. The stakes had risen too high for the other two. They watched as the Consul faced Rome's leading charioteer across the table. Scorpus was sweating and continually wiping his hands on his tunic. He'd gone in for more than he meant to and was 500,000 sesterces down to Flavius. He took another slug of wine from his cup, tried to put it down on the table, missed and it clattered to the floor. Nobody bent to pick it up.

'Double or quits then,' his voice was a little slurred. He stared at Flavius whose fat belly rested on the rim of the table. He wasn't going to allow this slob to break him, Scorpus, the great champion of the circus.

Flavius looked up. His sunken eyes shone like black beads out of a flabby face. 'You're pushing it a bit, aren't you? I didn't know charioteers could afford to lose a million.' He sat back on his chair. There was a hint of mockery in his voice.

'Damn you, Flavius, double or quits!'

'How are you going to pay if you lose?'

'The Emperor pays well. He likes us blues to win. He'll see me right if necessary.'

'The Emperor?' sneered Flavius. 'You must be mad if you think he'll bail you out. All he does is take money from other people.'

'You seem to have a low opinion of your cousin.' Flavius shrugged and picked up the dice. In a flash Scorpus brought down a dagger hard into the table top. It juddered in the wood between them.

'Not your dice, Flavius. I've had enough of those. We'll try our chances with Minicius's.' He pulled the other's leather pouch towards him and spilled out the dice, six red and six white.

'In that case,' said Flavius, 'Minicius can throw the dice. You do realise, I'm only giving you a chance. If you lose I want a million or that mansion of yours at Terracina. Is that agreed?'

'You'll get your bloody money.'

Minicius picked up the dice. 'Which colour do you choose, Flavius?'

'I'll take the red.'

'Are you happy with the white?' Minicius looked at Scorpus who nodded surlily. 'You don't want to test them?'

'Why should I? I've played with them enough times before. Let's get on.'

'Very well. It's double or quits for 500,000. One throw of the dice. What are you calling, Flavius?'

'Two eagles, one ram, one skull and two blanks. Write it on the block please, Polemus. I don't want any arguments.'

Scorpus picked up the white dice, turning them over. Two of the fingers on his left hand were missing, a legacy from a race a couple of years previously when they had been severed as his horses dragged him round the arena after he fell from his chariot. At length he said, 'One eagle, one ram, two skulls, one blank and one dog.' He shoved the dice over to Minicius. Polemus made a note on the writing block and read the bets back to them.

Minicius placed the white and red dice in two separate piles in front of him. He picked one from each pile, shook them about in his fist and threw them across the table. The white die showed the hare and the red one a blank. Flavius had scored one for a blank but Scorpus had got nothing for the hare. In the next two throws Flavius scored an eagle and a ram, making his total three. Scorpus won two points with a blank and a ram. Minicius shook again. This time the white die fell on the floor – it showed a skull. Scorpus had drawn level unless Flavius also scored. His die showed a hare.

'Do you want to go on with this?' leered Flavius. Scorpus made a grab for the dagger but Polemus was too quick for him. The weapon clanged on the marble floor and Polemus put his foot over it.

'Don't be a fool, Scorpus. Even you wouldn't get away with stabbing a consul.'

Scorpus sat down again. 'I'm not afraid of you, Flavius, or your money.' He motioned to Minicius. 'Roll the dice, will you?'

Minicius did as he was bid. This time the red die showed a dog and the white die another hare. Neither had scored.

'What do I need?' muttered Scorpus.

Polemus looked at his block. 'You want an eagle, another skull or a dog.'

Flavius leaned forward. 'I need another eagle, a skull or a blank, don't I?' Polemus nodded.

Minicius picked up the last two dice and cupped his hands around them. They rattled until he suddenly dropped them on the table. The white die spun on one of its corners and then settled. It showed a blank. The red die fell to show a skull. Flavius had won by four points to three.

Scorpus crashed his fist on the table in disgust and shouted to the door slave to bring his cloak. Flavius rubbed his hands with glee. A trickle of wine had run out of his mouth and dripped onto his tunic, staining it. 'Let me have the money in a week or I'll have you sold up, my dear Scorpus.' The latter lunged at his opponent but Minicius and Polemus restrained him, before leading him through the atrium and out into the street.

★ ★ ★

Crispinus was being carried through the busy Forum. He was in a sour mood made worse with the occasional jolt given to his chair by the crowds of people hurrying past. Domitian had returned from Albanum and Crispinus knew that it would not be long before he was summoned to the palace to report progress. The trouble was that there was nothing to report. He had heard no whispers or rumours of conspiracies against the Emperor's life. If necessary he would have to 'obtain' some evidence. Otherwise his own neck might be on the block. As he passed the colossal gilded statue of the Emperor on horseback, which in recent years had dominated the square, he found a slave walking alongside him.

'Crispinus, sir' the slave shouted to him, 'I am the slave of Scorpus, the charioteer. He asks if you would care to share a dish of flamingos' tongues with him in the Basilica Aemilia.'

Crispinus looked irritably at the slave. 'And why should I do that?'

'Sir, my master says that he has important information for you. Information that might be profitable for both of you.'

Crispinus considered for a moment. His visit to the

temple of Saturn to consult some records could wait. He told the slave to conduct him to Scorpus who was waiting by a food stall in the portico. Crispinus noticed that apart from the slave Scorpus was by himself and had draped a hood over his head, presumably to avoid being recognised.

Scorpus poured some mulled wine from a jug and pushed the plate of flamingo tongues across the table. He leaned over to Crispinus. 'I understand you may be looking for information. I have something that may be of great interest to you.' He stopped and ate a handful of tongues.

'Well,' said Crispinus, 'What is it? I can't spend all day gossiping here.'

'Ah,' Scorpus wiped his fingers on his tunic, 'it's not as simple as that. I'd want a bit of money. A bit of a deal, you see, between you and me.'

Crispinus laughed. 'By the gods, Scorpus, you've got a nerve. I could have you arrested now by the praetorians and worked over. They'd make you sing for nothing. Why should I pay you a penny?'

'I don't think the Emperor would appreciate his favourite charioteer being "worked over" as you put it. My information concerns him. Do you want a deal or not?'

'Very well, you say that this information may be profitable to us both. I propose we split anything I get for it from the Emperor.'

'How would I know what you got?'

'You can always ask him, Scorpus. I'm sure he'll tell his favourite charioteer.'

★ ★ ★

The guards gave him a sharp push, he lost his balance and Flavius Clemens's plump body slid across the floor of the great hall on the Palatine. He turned his head and saw the Emperor seated on a throne set upon the dais. On each side of the throne supported by bronze satyrs stood vast urns of white carystian marble burning incense from which smoke curled up to the barrel vault above.

Flavius felt the manacles bite into his wrists as he struggled to a kneeling position. 'My lord and god,' his throat was so tight that he could hardly speak. 'I beg you to tell me what I have done wrong and give me an opportunity to put it right.'

'But of course, my dear Flavius. That's why we've arranged this little interview.' The Emperor was standing over him now. He dared not raise his eyes but stared down at the leather boots a few inches from his face.

Domitian was speaking again. 'And you were doing so well as Consul, keeping all the senators from getting above themselves. I've always thought of you as one of my right hand men, you know, and now this.' Flavius glimpsed the Emperor's upturned palm point towards a figure standing by one of the columns. He recognised the lean figure of Regulus, a leader at the bar, who had prosecuted Arulenus to his death a few years previously. Behind him were grouped a claque of bravo callers to cheer him on whenever he made a point.

'You'll remember Regulus, of course. They say he makes straight for the throat and hangs onto it.' The latter smiled and inclined his head slightly at the Emperor's compliment. In his hand he held a scroll and next to him lolled a scribe with a sheaf of notes.

'My lord and god, please, I have no idea what I have done wrong. May I know the charges, please and seek the advice of my own counsel? I should like Gaius Plinius to defend me.'

'Oh, but I'm afraid that won't be possible. You see, we're short of time. And in any case Plinius is tied up in a lengthy trial at the Centumviral court. I happen to know because it's all about Helvidius who seems to have forgotten a legacy to me in his will.' The Emperor turned about and strode back to his throne. In the middle of that wide expanse of marble pavement, in silence, Flavius knelt alone. A side door opened and Scorpus, accompanied by a guard, slid into the chamber.

'Proceed if you will, Regulus.' The Emperor's voice echoed down the colonnades which lined each side of the hall. Regulus took a few steps forward. He was of middle age with a bronze coloured beard which did nothing to disguise the venom in his voice when speaking of the accused or his unctuous tones when he addressed the Emperor.

'My lord and god, the crimes of this defendant are so numerous that I have had to list them.' He indicated the scroll in his hand. 'It is especially distressing for us your loyal subjects to find a man closely related to your divine self and who has received so many honours from your generous hands behaving in such a treacherous manner.' The chorus master raised his hand and the claque behind him groaned in unison until he lowered it again. 'I shall enumerate the outrages committed by this cursed man,' here he pointed a gnarled finger at Flavius who had sunk onto his haunches, 'only briefly, in the hope that he will recognise his guilt immediately.' Regulus paused again and turned to his clerk who held the notes.

'The first count on the indictment is that the accused failed on numerous occasions to take the auspices before commencing business in the Senate.' The claque booed and followed their chorus master by jabbing their fingers in the direction of Flavius. 'The indications are, my lord and god, that the former Consul has no interest in the religions of the state. Indeed there is evidence that he has practised the black arts of the Jews or Christians.' A simulated gasp issued from the claque.

'I have never heard of such scandalous behaviour in a senator, let alone a member of the imperial family.' The mouth of the Emperor set in an angry line.

'My lord and god, I'm afraid I must burden you with further details of this wretch's treacherous conduct. I have to tell you that in the atrium of his house on the Quirinal a bust of the assassin Brutus was found.'

A tremor passed across the face of the Emperor and he gripped the gilded curlicues on each side of his seat. 'Are you saying that the accused has republican sympathies?' The words hissed from his mouth.

Regulus assumed an expression of the utmost grief. 'My lord, what other inference can one draw?' His bravo callers emitted a chorus of 'Ohs!' and covered their faces with their hands. He consulted his notes again. At the back of the hall a centurion of the Praetorian Guard and four soldiers filed in.

'The accused,' continued Regulus, 'was playing at dice for money when………..'

'Playing at dice?' roared Domitian, 'but that is illegal.'

Flavius raised his hand. 'The divine Augustus used to play, even in his litter.'

'I note the accused does not deny the offence,' went on Regulus smoothly. 'Your loyal subject and champion, Scorpus, is here to give evidence to prove it. He will tell you, my lord and god, that the accused defamed you foully during the game, suggesting that you steal money from innocent citizens.' Cries of 'Shame! Shame!' emanated from the chorus behind him.

The Emperor raised his hand. 'I have heard enough. This is the worst case of disloyalty that one could imagine. I know that you have further counts on the indictment relating to the accused's immorality, but I do not need to hear them. Guards!'

Flavius Clemens was handled roughly to his feet. The soldiers stood round him with their swords drawn. As the Emperor began to speak he fell again to his knees. The centurion grabbed his hair and jerked him upright.

'Unshackle him. He will need the use of his hands soon enough.' One of the soldiers produced a key and released the link to the fetter on one wrist. 'Now Flavius, I should not wish you to think I was unmerciful. You know the traditional method of execution; tying to a stake and flogging till you stop breathing. Your status saves you from that and I will not have you strangled like a common prisoner. Do you have any preference?'

'My lord and god, if I might be allowed to take poison?'

'Very well, but you must be dead by sunset. Norbanus.' The Prefect of the Guard, his face expressionless, stepped forward from behind a pillar where he had remained unseen. 'You have heard the sentence. See to it that the accused commits suicide as instructed.' Without a word Norbanus inclined his head and gave a sharp order to the centurion. The Emperor took an apple from a tray beside him and began to eat it.

CHAPTER VII

INITIATION

Every day at first light Domitilla called for her litter to carry her down into the Field of Mars. Near the old sheep market stood the Iseum on the pediment of which was sculpted a statue of the goddess Isis, riding on a hound. She climbed the steps to be greeted by the shaven-headed priest in his white linen robe. As he sprinkled her head and hands, the water from the stoup made her shiver in the cool air of the early morning. In the shadows of the interior another priest drew back the curtain to unveil the goddess and clothe her in a jewelled robe for the day. Domitilla joined the choirs which lined both sides of the shallow flight of steps at the top of which the precentor waited between two lions of basalt. He carried a sacred vase inside his robe while two acolytes gently fanned the air with palm leaves. Somewhere in the smoky gloom she heard the rhythmic beat of the sistrum and the timbrel. The traditional lamentations of Isis began. On Domitilla's side the choir represented the goddess herself. Opposite they chanted the replies of Nephthys, her sister. Alternately the passion of Osiris was enacted between the two. At the base of the steps on the great marble table engraved by Neilos glowed the sacred fire. The interpreter of dreams stepped slowly forward, holding aloft a white staff in his right hand and a flask of frankincense in the other. At the end of each verse he scattered incense on the embers. His body began to sway to the rhythm of the music, and the aromatic fumes, fanned by the palm leaves, wafted over the heads of the singers.

Domitilla was intoxicated by the atmosphere. She clasped the hand of her neighbour on each side as the whole choir sang in unison to celebrate the resurrection of the river god and the birth of Horus. The timbrel faded and a single flute sounded a few sorrowful notes to mark the end of the lamentation. The notes floated away into the recesses of the cornice while the beat of the sistrum grew more insistent, faster. The choirs clapped and swayed to the holy fire flaring under the waving fronds of palm. The priest chanted in couplets a prayer to Isis to which the worshippers responded. The precentor removed the sacred vase from his robe and, holding it before him, descended the steps scattering drops of symbolic Nile water over the heads of the singers. When he reached the bottom all fell silent. He knelt before the uncovered statue of the goddess to place the vase at her feet. With the others, Domitilla took a barley cake from the basket held by the acolyte and laid it by the vase, so that the goddess might have food and drink for the coming day.

Often Domitilla walked back to the Palatine on foot, escorted only by a freedman. She draped a shawl about her head to avoid being recognised and followed the bend in the Tiber as it looped towards the island with its temple dedicated to Aesculapius and the bridge nearby which, according to legend, Horatius had held against the Etruscan hordes of Lars Porsenna. The dark waters of the river flowed slowly and soothingly. Domitilla did not hurry to return to a palace which housed only fear and whispers. After the death of Flavius Clemens she had thought of retreating to her villa at Reate but Marciana had advised against it. She must think of her children. Any move on her part which could be interpreted as disloyalty to the Emperor might prove dangerous for them. She had written privately to the camp in Germany imploring Trajan not to let the boys leave, but had not dared to use the imperial post, feeling sure that any letter written by her would be intercepted and opened. Trajan had not replied and she wondered anxiously whether he had received her letter. The boys would know in any event of their father's suicide. She grieved for them, but not for herself. Any feelings for her husband had died long before him. It was a relief that the boys would grow up away from a father who had shown little affection and done nothing for them, preferring instead a dissolute existence of his own. She reproached herself for failing as a wife and mother. Perhaps she could have saved her marriage. Now she could not even bring herself to mourn Clemens, however shameful the treatment he had received. Their family life had been so empty. She longed to have loved and nurtured her sons as Isis had cared for Horus. Instead she was remote from them. Did they ever think of her while they learned the art of soldiery in the dark mists and pine forests by the banks of the Rhine?

One day she walked up past the mausoleum of the divine Augustus. The golden eagles perched high on their pillars around the tomb glittered in the morning sun. Just beyond, she reached the Altar of Peace set up by the Emperor nearly ninety years ago. On the sparkling marble walls the frieze of life-size figures processed to mark the dedication of the altar. Here was the Emperor with his loving family gathered together. She found Agrippa and his son, young Gaius Caesar, a protective hand laid upon his head, perhaps by Drusus. Next to him the Empress Livia stood, followed by the tiny Lucius holding his mother's hand. Domitilla stretched up to caress the chubby features of the little boy upon whose chest rested a medallion not unlike her own. The men wore olive wreaths and priestly gowns. None smiled but gazed reflectively, some forwards to the future, some back into the past. A deep melancholy infused their faces. Had the sculptor foreseen the tragedies that were to strike this family and ironically chiselled them into this intended symbol of a new beginning, a new era of health and happiness? Poor Gaius and Lucius Caesar, adopted by their grandfather soon after their birth and groomed for the principate, had both died young, one in suspicious circumstances. Was this the fate that awaited her own two boys, adopted by an emperor and doomed to die as well? She turned away and called to Stephanus to escort her home. She must pray again to Isis, the guardian of the family. From the cloudy waters of the river she felt the spirit of Osiris well up around her. She thought again of the shrine on the hill and of Hispo. She longed for him to fill her loneliness.

When the precentor of the temple saw how devoted Domitilla had become to the goddess he asked her if she wished to be initiated into the solemn mysteries. He knew that she was the niece of the Emperor who had caused the Iseum to be substantially restored a few years previously. The rites of initiation were however secret and she must tell nobody of her experiences.

A few days later, as the sun disappeared behind the Janiculum hill Domitilla presented herself at the temple. She took off her gown and handed it to Orestilla to take back to the palace. A female acolyte dressed her in a simple linen surplice and led her to a small chamber off the main body of the temple. 'Here,' the acolyte said, 'you must sleep the night and this is your pillow.' She indicated a log of polished cedar wood which lay on the floor beside a woollen rug. On a table lay a bronze platter with a small loaf on it. Beside it stood an earthenware pitcher of water.

'Eat the loaf without the water before you go to sleep. You may not eat again until the ceremonies are over. The interpreter of dreams will come at the midnight hour. Do not fear him. He will not speak or touch you; he will stand beside where you are lying for a few minutes and then leave.'

The door to the chamber closed and Domitilla was alone. In a niche she saw by the light of the solitary candle a painted statue of Isis. Around the feet of the goddess the paint had worn away to reveal the bare marble where lips had pressed against it. She knelt for a moment on the stone floor and then lay down on the mat to sleep.

In the morning the acolyte came again and led her to the priest of the door. Three times he doused her hands and head in the sacred water, for she must be cleansed and fasted in preparation for the evening. The day before, Domitilla had brought with her from the palace eyes and ears of jewelled silk. These she now laid before the unveiled statue of the goddess, symbols of her ability to see and hear all things. She was given extracts from the hieratic books to read and told that she must remain beside the statue until the moon had risen.

At about the sixth hour an old man wearing papyrus shoes sat down next to her. 'I am the interpreter of dreams,' he said. 'Did you know that you had a dream last night?'

'I have no recollection of a dream and I slept well.'

'Indeed you were sleeping very peacefully when I came into your cell. But I listened to your mind and I saw the shadow of your future slip away through the silvery darkness of the window.'

Domitilla looked at the old man. He had a shrivelled face and a toothless smile. His unkempt hair hung in straggles round a scrawny neck. 'Do you know what I dreamed of then?' she asked.

'I saw a ship and a voyage by sea.' He looked up at the statue of the goddess and tapped his stick on the marble pavement. Then he said, as if it related to something quite different, 'You will not find what you are looking for, not here, not yet. One day you will find it and only you will know and understand.' He scrambled to his feet and without another word he shuffled away. Domitilla listened to his stick tapping as he descended the steps out of the temple and emerged into the sunlight streaming through the pillars of the portico. The she-cats lay curled up asleep beneath a shelf containing scrolls in wooden cases. The silence was broken by the occasional slap of a priest's sandals on the floor as he attended to some office. Otherwise all was quiet.

At last the light began to fade. A new priest came and held out a crimson robe for Domitilla to step into. Eight girls, wearing long white dresses and each with a single lotus flower in her hair, began a ritual dance to the sound of an unseen timbrel. Ribbons fluttered and in each hand they held a lighted taper. They circled round Domitilla standing in their midst so that it seemed as if she were adorned by a diadem of sparkling jewels. The young girls were chanting a hymn in praise of the goddess, rejoicing in the lights of Isis. Sometimes they pressed close to her, touching the robe, only to retreat barefooted to gather round the statue of the goddess, kneeling and throwing up their hands in supplication. Somewhere strong incense was burning. Domitilla began to feel a little faint. Two hands gently took her elbows offering support. From the shadows of the colonnade the precentor appeared bearing the vase of sacred water wrapped inside his robe. He was followed by an acolyte round whose left arm was coiled a golden asp with its lobes dilated and its sphinx-like head held high. Behind him walked a priestess with long braided hair. In her left hand she shook the sistrum in time to the beat of the timbrel. Their white surplices glinted in the light of the tapers and of a bright lamp carved in the shape of a boat carried by a man who now came to stand before Domitilla. On his head he wore the mask of a dog and in his left hand he clasped a herald's wand. This was Anubis, ferryman of dead souls to the underworld and the companion and messenger of Isis in her quest to find the body of Osiris.

Gently the two hands at her elbows propelled her forwards. Domitilla followed the procession up the steps towards the sanctuary beyond. The high entrance was formed by two granite obelisks covered in Egyptian signs incomprehensible to her. At the door the priest of Anubis turned to face her, inclined his head and motioned with his wand that she should enter. At first Domitilla could make out nothing, for the only light came from the embers of a fire consuming the incense she had smelt earlier. The air was warm and seemed to cling to her in the thick atmosphere. She heard the mournful sound of a lyre being plucked, with long pauses between the notes, as Isis wept for her dead husband. A cup of wine was placed in her hands and someone whispered in her ear, 'Drink. This is the water of the Nile, the water of life from which all goodness flows.' She took a sip. The wine was strong and sweet. She tried to lower the cup but a hand came out of the darkness and held it fast to her lips. She was forced to drain it. Her head began to swim. Somewhere in front of her she detected the dark form of a mummy swathed in linen bands and lying on a couch. From its thighs a phallus protruded starkly upwards. Behind her, beyond the confines of the sanctuary, she could hear the priestess singing a soft dirge. The wine, the warmth, the rhythm of the sistrum, the plangent notes of the lyre, the melancholy singing and the dim light all combined to induce in Domitilla a sense of well-being and drowsiness. She felt the robe slip from her shoulders as her two supporters drew it from her and with it gently wafted the air, in simulation of the wings of Isis creating the Etesian winds. Slowly, almost imperceptibly, the mummy rose from its prostrate position on the couch. The life blood flowed back into Osiris as the mummy stood before her. She stepped forwards and the phallus rested for a moment comfortably between her thighs. The resurrection and the consummation were fulfilled. She had become a priestess of Isis.

They dressed her in a marriage veil of saffron with a silver moon upon her head. In her left hand she carried a ewer of gold while in her right arm she cradled a cornucopia filled with sheaves of corn. The swollen throat of the serpent rose from her forehead and before her walked Anubis, his staff held high in celebration. Outside the sanctuary the young girls broke into a chorus of rejoicing and tossed lotus flowers at her feet. Domitilla blinked nervously in the strong light. An acolyte proffered to her a plate of walnuts and quail eggs to break her fast.

CHAPTER VIII

AMPHITHEATRE

Spring advanced into summer. The Emperor, still harbouring presentiments of his own death, went to Cumae to consult the Sybil there. He took with him a new mistress whom he had spotted in the amphitheatre while presiding over a gladiatorial contest between dwarves and women. The courtiers and freedmen on the Palatine relaxed a little.

Taking advantage of the Emperor's absence, Domitilla walked down into the garden of the stadium. The sun was approaching its zenith and shone directly into the secluded court. Already she could hear the honeybees at work among the flowers. The gravel crunched beneath her feet as she walked with Orestilla along the path beside the central canal above which ran a pergola entwined with roses. At intervals the water was spanned by bridges of yellow marble on whose parapets boys rode astride leaping dolphins. From her altar bisecting the canal the goddess Minerva gazed over the topiary of myrtle and box cut into fantastic shapes of centaurs, ships at sea, lions and even monkeys dangling from branches. Beyond the low-trimmed hedges lining the path, bronze urns threw up sprays of colour: the deep indigo of lavender, pale lilies to contrast with poppies of magenta, beds of acanthus and the silvery leaves of Jupiter's beard trimmed into the shape of globes, competing with the white and pink of oleander. Amid this profusion a gilded Hercules wrestled with snaky-headed Hydra and Artemis fired her bow at a fleeing stag.

They reached the end of the path and sat down on a curved marble bench. Behind them from a niche of aquamarine mosaics emerged Silanus clasping a waterskin. Its contents trickled down rough-hewn rocks into the basin of a fountain round the rim of which perched sculptured ibis and herons. Thrushes flapped among the bushes and a frog disappeared with a light plop from a lily pad into the canal. Occasionally the two women rose to do a turn along the paths. It was a convenient and pleasant way of taking exercise. They sat afterwards under a parasol, enjoying the tranquillity and watching the lizards basking, like them, in the high sun.

The sound of footsteps on the gravel woke Domitilla from her doze. Before her stood Nereus carrying a small diptych sealed with a signet ring whose design she did not recognise. She broke open the seal and read the message on the wax inside. It was from Hispo saying that he had returned to Rome and would be glad if she would visit him at his apartment in the Golden House.

'How did you receive this, Nereus?'

'My lady, I was in the vegetable market. A man approached me saying that he believed I was your freedman. I told him that was so and he handed me the case, asking me to deliver it to you immediately. He said he would wait for me tomorrow outside the amphitheatre at the ninth hour to see if there was a reply.'

Domitilla looked down at the letters incised upon the wax. She had been waiting for it; yet it came as a shock. Her hands were trembling and she closed the diptych with a snap.

'Thank you, Nereus. There's no reply at the moment.'

'My lady,' Nereus inclined his head, 'is there anything else?'

'No, no, you may go now.' Domitilla raised her hand slightly in a gesture of dismissal and Nereus turned to leave, but then she added, 'Smoothe this wax and make sure the words are obliterated completely.' She handed back the diptych.

The following day, however, in the shadow of the conical fountain Nereus met the man who had approached him in the market and told him his mistress would come at the appointed place in the afternoon of the next day. A retired legionary who had been washing his face in the water of the fountain followed at a distance as the messenger from Hispo walked away.

★ ★ ★

Domitilla's litter, carried by four sturdy Germans, stopped at the main entrance to the Palatine on the Via Triumphalis. A praetorian guard handed to Orestilla a disc giving entrance to the Golden House. As they climbed the slope of the Esquiline hill Domitilla glimpsed through the curtains the colossal statue of Nero towering over the Forum. Round its base lay garlands of flowers and from the giant head, which her grandfather had thoughtfully replaced with an image of the sun, radiated a gleaming aureole of golden spikes. Soon they reached the pentagonal court lined with colonnades at the front of the vast palace which Nero had built for himself. Much of it lay in ruins and the rest was deserted. Domitilla stepped out, instructing Orestilla to return in three hours and then to wait, if necessary. A caretaker came forward to conduct her into the hall of the golden vault. Some of the stucco had fallen away from the walls but the pavement still shone in the dusty sunlight which illuminated triangular and rhomboid tiles of ivory-white marble interspersed with glass of red, green and azure. On a plinth the Trojan priest Laocöon and his two sons struggled with the sea serpents sent to crush them to death as a punishment for warning the citizens of Troy against driving the wooden horse into the city. Domitilla remembered, as a small girl, gazing up at the anguished face of the father whose veined muscles swelled in the deadly contest with the suffocating coils of the monsters while his sons tried unsuccessfully to free their own smooth young bodies. She turned away and hurried through to the long passage at the back of the palace. It was hard to see, for some of the windows in the barrel vault fifteen feet above her head had been blocked up. She started as a cobweb wrapped itself around her face and she caught a whiff of sulphur in the dank air. High up in the gloom the channel, now dry, which had brought water in a cascade to the octagon, hung like a suspended arch. A crack of daylight and a narrow flight of steps signalled the far end of the dusty corridor. There Hispo stepped out from a small doorway to one side and she almost fell into his arms. He held her for a moment and kissed her lightly on the cheek. She felt a little breathless.

'Oh, that passage used to be so light,' she laughed nervously as he led her into a simple room. It was furnished with a wooden table and two chairs. On the table lay the remains of a meal of cheese and lettuce, with some burnt bread in a basket to freshen the air. Propped in a corner Domitilla saw his wooden sword, the symbol of a gladiator's freedom, and on a nail hung a bronze helmet. There were no rugs on the floor. For a moment each stood there uncertainly. To break the awkwardness she pointed to the helmet and asked if she could look at it. He took it from its peg and placed it on the table. The crest was shaped like a fish and around the outside were embossed the figures of wild animals, panthers and lions springing at their prey. From each side and at the back large flanges protruded. Domitilla saw that they were gouged where the swords or pikes of opponents had struck. Beneath was a grill to protect the face. She bent to pick it up and grimaced at the weight. Inside, the leather lining was stained black with sweat. She thought she detected the smell of blood. Hispo replaced the helmet and took her by the hand.

'Let's find somewhere to sit. My rooms are rather sparse and crude for a member of the imperial family used to living on the Palatine.'

'Don't forget I used to live here for many years, though it was a bit different in those days.'

'Why did you come along that dark passage?'

'I thought it was a bit more discreet than walking through the colonnade at the front.'

Hispo nodded and they walked up a short flight of steps leading to a tiny courtyard cut into the side of the hill. Domitilla looked up and recognised the small temple of Fortuna on the slope above. Its translucent stone from Asia glittered like a jewel in the sun. Her mother had once taken her inside to show how the daylight penetrated even when the doors were closed, so that the inscriptions on the walls could still be read. Now the grass surrounding it was overgrown and the path leading to it had disappeared.

For an hour or more they sat and talked. It was not long before the easy intimacy of the shrine overlooking the lake at Albanum had been rekindled. Hispo was busy with the troupe of gladiators he was training for a show in the amphitheatre to take place at the end of the month. The Emperor's gladiators had to be the best; they had to win or Hispo would answer for their failure. He hoped he would be allowed to retire completely afterwards. 'If my tiros do well the Emperor may not allow me to retire. If they fight badly,

I shall probably be punished.' He paused and then took Domitilla's hand in his. 'You are brave to come here, especially after what happened to Clemens. Domitian is in a dangerous mood.'

'I don't fear for myself really. It's my sons I worry about. At the moment I think they're safe with Trajan in Germany.'

'What's the atmosphere like on the Palatine?'

'Nobody ever speaks of the Emperor. Everybody's terrified that anything they say will be repeated to him. He's away at Cumae for a few days but his spies are everywhere. He's convinced that people are plotting against him all the time. I'm sure that's why Clemens was forced to commit suicide. He hadn't done anything wrong – it was just to frighten others.'

'Do you ever speak to the Empress?'

'Oh, Domitia just puts up with him. At one time I think she was genuinely fond of him. Now his excesses frighten her like everybody else. We get on very well together but I'm careful what I talk about. She says that all Domitian is interested in is his archery and any other woman but her. She thinks he's rather pathetic.'

'I think he's become capricious and cruel, like Nero. The other day he had a spectator at the games dragged from his seat and torn to pieces by dogs, just because he overheard him saying that a Thracian might be a match for a Murmillo, but not for the Emperor. He can't stand even the slightest criticism. He's always been biased against Thracians.'

They sat on for a little while until Hispo had to go for the evening exercise of his trainees at the barracks. They agreed to meet again the following day, and for several days afterwards Domitilla's litter could be seen swaying up the hill to the deserted palace. Each afternoon they spent sitting in the little courtyard behind Hispo's rooms. Domitilla loved the simplicity and peace. Here she was not watched and they could speak freely to each other. When the time came to return to the Palatine she often lingered, wandering into the rooms and halls she had known in her childhood and later when she was bringing up the boys. She found a box of their toys in the nursery where the floor was a mosaic map of the city after much of it had been rebuilt following the terrible fire. In the box were some knuckle bones and a pair of tiny military cloaks which the family nurse, Phyllis, had made for them. On a shelf lay the harp which her uncle Titus had given to her when he was teaching her to play. She tried to pluck it but the strings crumbled in her fingers.

Sometimes she strayed a little further, through the passages and rooms of the imperial suite, where the walls were decorated with white stucco divided into panels by delicate lines of filigreed tracery draped with ivy and vine leaves. In the panels appeared mythological scenes or groups of birds and animals. Many of the bedroom walls were still studded with pearls and in one she discovered a painting of Nero's wife, Poppaea, clearly recognisable by her amber hair and face kept pale by bathing in the milk of she-asses. Domitilla shuddered at the thought of this poor woman being kicked to death by a man who was supposed to love her. What kind of monster could do that and then order Famulus to paint her portrait for his bedroom?

One afternoon she went as usual to Hispo's rooms. He was waiting for her in the courtyard and they sat under a fig tree which had seeded itself in a crack in the pavement. She thought he seemed a little quieter than normal and once or twice she caught in his eyes a trace of anxiety which she had never noticed before. She asked if there was anything wrong but he simply shook his head and smiled. Perhaps, she thought, he is worried about the games and his troupe of gladiators. He drained his cup of watered wine, stood up and put out both his hands to her.

'Come inside. I have something I want to give you.' She waited by the wooden table while he disappeared for a moment into the back. When he returned he was carrying a small leather cloth which he unwrapped. Inside lay a silver ring encasing a cameo of sardonyx showing a sacred lotus flower in relief. 'I found this in a jeweller's shop in the Argiletum. I thought it might be suitable for a priestess of Isis.' He took her hand and gently pressed the ring onto her finger. It fitted well.

Domitilla trembled in the half-light of the sparse room. She felt overwhelmed by a surge of happiness and love for this strong and simple man. She gazed down at the white and yellow stone and the rough but kind hand which still held hers. He put his arms round her waist and rubbed his nose gently in her hair. She felt a tear trickle onto her forehead. Looking up she saw that he was weeping and instinctively she pulled him towards her. Her hands began to play up and down his back and she opened her mouth as his lips found hers. She pulled his buttocks into her thighs and felt his hardness like the mummy of Osiris in the temple. In his little bedroom they gave themselves completely to each other.

When it was time for Domitilla to leave, Hispo held her very tightly, kissing her on the forehead, the eyes and then the lips. He stroked her hair while she clasped him round the waist and held her head against his bare chest. They would meet, he said, in a few days, after the games. He would send a message. She touched his sad eyes with her fingers and he kissed the ring on her finger. They lingered in each other's arms, postponing the inevitable goodbye.

When she reached the end of the passage Domitilla hesitated. The ninth hour was approaching but the litter could wait. She wanted to rest in the old palace where once she had been happy and where she felt close to the man whose love now filled her mind and body. Was it not the lotus flower which induced a feeling of dreamy forgetfulness and an unwillingness to depart? Who had told her that? She could not remember. Her foot dislodged a loose tile as she went to sit down on a bench. Somewhere above her head an owl, disturbed by the noise, flapped away, its mournful cry echoing through the eerie vaults and porticoes. Startled from her reverie Domitilla stumbled into another chamber. The elaborately decorated ceiling seemed familiar, and dimly she remembered being told by her grandfather that here Nero had declaimed his epic poem on the Trojan War and sung many of his ballads. She peered up at the faded painting of Hector taking leave of Andromache outside the walls of the city, before his struggle to the death with Achilles. The artist had portrayed the warrior with his long spear, drawing back from the outstretched arms of his wife. His face was etched with melancholy and the ineluctability of fate which her tear-stained longing could do nothing to assuage. Domitilla sensed the pathos in both figures and remembered the tears of Hispo which she had not understood.

Her litter was waiting beneath the colonnade. The sun shone through the tiered arches of the Aqua Claudia whose high pillars cast long shadows like a giant's fingers over the surrounding buildings. She gave orders to be carried to the temple of Isis which she reached in time for the last service of the day. The choirs had lit boat-shaped lamps which they held in their hands as they chanted and said lauds in praise of the goddess. Afterwards Domitilla moved forward with the precentor to disrobe the statue and veil it with curtains for the night. In the sanctuary she prayed first to the mummy of

Osiris for the safety of her sons and that she might bring happiness to Hispo. The fragrance of burnt myrrh hung in the air and with its black and yellow eyes a she-cat watched unblinking as she knelt and fumbled for the words of supplication to the goddess, her protectress. At length the holder of the keys came to lock the doors and Domitilla rode back to the Palatine. The Emperor had returned. The palace lay hushed and cowed in the sultry air of early night.

★ ★ ★

It was the day which Domitian had appointed for the commencement of games to celebrate the opening of his third campaign in Pannonia and Upper Moesia. Domitilla awoke with a start to find Orestilla standing by her bed.

'My lady, Parthenius is at the door with a message from the Emperor.'

'At this hour? Ask him to wait please. I will see him once I'm dressed.'

'My lady, he says that the matter cannot wait. He has instructions from the Emperor to speak to you immediately.'

'Very well. Fetch my shawl and slippers please. I will see him in the antechamber.'

When Domitilla entered the room she found Parthenius standing near the entrance talking to her freedman, Stephanus. He looked a trifle uncomfortable.

'Well? What does my lord and god desire that is so pressing?'

'My lady, I must apologise for disturbing you.' Parthenius was his usual courteous self. 'But the Emperor instructs me to inform you that he requires your attendance at the games today.' On seeing Domitilla enter, Parthenius had looked up. Now he was gazing at the floor as if ashamed of something.

'My attendance? Whatever for? The Emperor knows that it is not my habit to visit the amphitheatre.'

Parthenius shuffled and met her eyes at last. 'My lady, the Emperor offered no reason. He simply gave me the message and told me to inform you immediately. He did say that you need not attend the wild beast hunts this morning or the executions at lunchtime, but you are to be in the imperial box before the sixth hour when the gladiators fight.'

'Very well, if I must attend. Tell the Emperor that I will obey his orders even though he knows that I dislike these spectacles.'

'Did he say anything to you before I came in?' asked Domitilla when Parthenius had left.

'My lady,' replied Stephanus, 'he seemed a bit agitated. He's normally a pretty calm man even when the Emperor is having one of his fits of temper. He said the Emperor was stabbing flies on the wall outside his bedroom with a stylus and muttering to himself. Apparently that's a bad sign.'

Domitilla returned to her rooms and dressed for the visit to the amphitheatre. It was only the second time she had been since the completion of the colossal arena on the site of the old lake in front of the Golden House. She had often heard the roars of the crowd erupting across the deserted city as some gladiator or animal met his end in the blood-stained sand. Sometimes in the past, to avoid the disturbing sensation of guilt, she had taken herself off to the family estate at Reate and dallied there until whichever festival was taking place had finished. Today she had no choice but to attend. Perhaps she might spot Hispo in the crowd. She tried to comfort herself with this thought.

The people, in ragged brown streams, had converged from all sides on the entrances to the amphitheatre, past the street vendors selling sausages and pastries and the stalls which offered favours in support of one gladiator or another. Now only a few chairs and litters carrying senators, knights and their ladies swayed down the Via Sacra towards the cliff of luminescent marble which soared into a sky white with heat. A low hum emanated from the great bowl as the citizens of Rome contemplated their programmes and studied the form of the contestants. Outside an eerie quiet prevailed. Domitilla heard the shuffle of her bearers' sandals on the basalt pavement. From their niches in the walls of the theatre Greek and Roman gods and goddesses, emperors and generals gazed down balefully. High up, the bronze shields which Domitian had fixed to the uppermost tier shone like miniature suns. Above the canopy the air shimmered as the sweat poured from eighty thousand bodies. In the distance carts rumbled away down the deserted streets, bearing the corpses of criminals and the carcases of animals. The paw of a black bear trailed in the dust as it hung lifelessly from the back of a low wagon piled high with stinking flesh and fur. Some of the statues of gods and goddesses, veiled so that their eyes might not behold the lunchtime executions of criminals, were still being uncovered. Along the way the hoardings advertised the contests of the day in bold red or black lettering on white boards: 'See the son of Spiculus in his first fight in Rome;' 'Superbus will fight Hanno to the death' and 'Who will left-handed Alemannus meet in the arena?'

Orestilla caught her breath and pointed. 'My lady, do you see the sign on the wall above the Emperor's gateway?'

Domitilla lowered her fan of egret feathers and looked. Above the entrance Jupiter rode in a chariot drawn by four prancing horses. But next to the statue in letters much bigger than the other signs she read, 'Hermes fights here again today.'

She clutched at Orestilla's hand. 'Surely that can't be Hispo, can it? He has his freedom. He can't be made to fight now. He's too old!' Orestilla made no reply. They passed into the shadow of the amphitheatre. There was no going back.

The bearers set the litter down before the imperial gate. Domitilla stepped out, hardly knowing where she was. She felt a hand guide her forward and she began to mount the stairway leading to the podium. At the top sat the gaunt figure of Manlius Valens, almost ninety years old and trying to catch his breath. It was rumoured that Domitian intended to appoint this poor old man, nearly blind and deaf, to be a consul the following year; another calculated insult to the Senate. He stuttered a word of greeting to Domitilla as she passed and extended a bony hand, but she did not notice and he sank back exhausted.

A wall of heat and noise met her as she emerged into the light. With her fan she shaded her eyes and followed an attendant to a seat a few places away from the thrones which would be occupied by the Emperor and Domitia Longina. Slave boys, in white tunics laced with gold thread, gently wafted palm fronds to cool the air beneath a purple canopy that covered the imperial box. From time to time tiny jets sprayed a mist of scented water. Around her, senators and equestrians dressed in their white togas filled the lower ring. Opposite, on the far side of the arena, sat the consuls and the vestal virgins. Immediately beneath her feet a wall dropped thirteen feet to the freshly raked sand. From the top of this wall protruded iron spars to support the nets which had prevented the animals slaughtered in the morning from trying to escape. Behind and above, row upon row of steps rose, where the ordinary citizens in their grubby clothes contrasted sharply with the gleaming white of their superiors below. Still higher up sat the women and the slaves crammed together, while out of sight in the uppermost wooden gallery prostitutes plied their trade in the shady corners under the canopy.

From the seat behind Domitilla's Julia Frontina leaned forward to say something but her words were drowned in the great roar as the crowd rose to its feet and raised their right arms in salute. Domitian and the Empress moved slowly to their thrones of gilt and ivory. The Emperor wore a purple toga embroidered with silver thread. His wig was held in place by a golden diadem bearing the images of the Capitoline triad, Jupiter, Juno and Minerva. At his side walked a dwarf dressed in a red tunic. His head was disproportionately large and he rested it on the arm of the Emperor's throne where he stood beside him. Domitian settled himself, then looked round the imperial box, seeming to satisfy himself that Domitilla was present. A slave came forward with a dish of dates from which the Emperor selected two and fed them to the dwarf.

From a gateway to the left chariots entered the arena, each bearing one of the stars to perform that afternoon. Women screamed and waved bits of clothing as they recognised their favourites. The gladiators were bareheaded but sported gaily coloured cloaks. Behind each chariot walked slaves carrying their arms and armour ready to be tested before the fights began. At the approach of each chariot Domitilla fixed her eyes intently on the occupant. Again and again she searched; he was not there. She leaned back in her seat and closed her eyes – there must be some other Hermes that she had not recognised; and yet she knew it was not true. She felt a damp hand on her arm and looked down to see the hideous dwarf leering up at her. Domitian had turned in his seat and was watching both of them. The dwarf pointed to the gladiators' gateway. There stood Hispo in a black chariot drawn by two stallions. The citizens of Rome went wild as he acknowledged their cheers. Shouts of 'Hermes! Hermes!' reverberated round the arena. Behind the chariot a slave was carrying his armour and the helmet which she had seen in the Golden House. The dwarf chuckled and walked back to resume his position beside the Emperor's throne. Domitilla put up her fan to hide her face.

Once the parade was over the inspection of the weapons took place and lots were drawn to decide who would fight whom. On the far side of the arena some of the lesser known gladiators were warming up, thrusting their spears and blunted swords. In front of the imperial box the stars formed a line to greet the Emperor before the contests began. Hispo was among them, not thirty paces from her, but he did not look. She wondered if he realised she was present. He stood impassively, swathed in a red cloak with his pale hair swept back and fastened with a band across his forehead. His eyes were fixed upon the Emperor. Domitilla willed him to look aside at her. Surely he had seen her as he paraded in his chariot; still he gave no sign.

The individual fights began. In the blistering glare of the sunlight the gladiators seemed to Domitilla like black shadows darting on a stage of burnished silver. All colour was obliterated in the brightness. Her senses became numbed by the cacophony of noise, the fanfare of trumpets as Thracian faced Retiarius, and by the thunder of drums signalling the climax of a struggle when the crowd waited on the Emperor's decision. The screams and chants rolled down like avalanches from the tiered seats above. She could not think; she could not see. She was enveloped by a sickening foreboding. In her mind she sought to keep the image of her goddess, the serene presence of the little statue on the hill who could protect and heal, who could overcome the fates.

Into the ring strode Andax, a Samnite. His strong young torso glistened already with sweat. Round his waist he wore a thick studded belt, his forearms and thighs were strapped with bands of leather and his left shin was protected by a greave. He moved easily and confidently to the centre of the arena, holding aloft his oblong shield and shortsword. He pushed back his visored helmet to reveal his face and the crowd howled their support. Against his name in the programme appeared an M followed by three V's. The M meant that he had fought bravely in his first contest and been granted 'missio' by the president of the games, allowing him to leave the arena alive even though he had been defeated. The three V's indicated victory in each of his next fights. He was the coming star whom everybody feared.

Amidst the shouting Domitilla heard the water organ begin to play. The trumpeters pointed their instruments skywards and suddenly she saw him again. He emerged from the tunnel and walked steadily towards the Emperor's box, just as she had seen him that first day striding smoothly across the side of the hill. Her fear was stilled; here was a man like no other. She was alert now; all the numbness of the previous hour had melted away. From his helmet there rose a plume of fluttering red horsehair. His body was naked save for a leather skirt and a metal disc which covered his right shoulder. He carried a sword longer than the Samnite's, but his shield was round and smaller. The heralds held up signs to the crowd, 'Your hero Hermes fights again'. Men and women stood and waved their programmes, a sea of white arms surged upwards from the grubby tunics of the people to greet the champion of a decade past. Now he was standing before the pulvinar on which Domitian lounged. Hispo raised his arm and turned slowly round, requesting silence from the crowd. From the centre of the arena Andax watched and waited. Gradually the hubbub died away until nothing moved or sounded. Eighty thousand Romans strained their ears to listen. But Hispo did not turn to face the Emperor. He looked up to Domitilla. He spoke in a loud and clear voice.

'My lady, if I am to die today, please pray to your goddess that I may be granted a safe passage to the cool waters where Osiris dwells. I take my leave of you and I salute you with my body and my soul.'

Domitilla's fingers bit like teeth into the arms of her seat and she leaned forward inclining her head in silent acknowledgment. For a moment their eyes held each other's. Hispo turned away and bowed almost perfunctorily to the Emperor who did not respond. Domitilla stared straight ahead, fighting to keep her emotions in check and deprive the Emperor of the pleasure of witnessing her pain. She felt Julia Frontina's arm around her shoulders, before it was hastily removed under Domitian's glare. The dwarf sniggered and swallowed another date. There was a murmur round the imperial box soon drowned by the baying roars of the mob. Hermes, the veteran, was facing the new superstar, Andax.

'Why does Hermes wear so little armour?' Julia asked her husband, Senecio.

'He's probably trying to preserve his speed and agility by carrying very little weight. Andax must be fitter and faster. They say that Hermes was only told a week ago that he would have to fight. He cannot be ready for the arena, but he knows a trick or two.'

The two men circled round each other, probing and testing the other's defence. The crowd urged them to come to grips but Andax gradually gave ground at every clash of shields and swords. He knew he would last the longer of the two; Hermes must tire and the chance to strike would come. Andax was lighter on his feet and slimmer too. Hermes had the more muscular body but he was heavier. Time was on the side of his younger opponent. The crowd grew restless, for Andax continued to stand off, darting backwards or sideways, anything to keep Hermes on the move. Domitilla saw his chest begin to heave as his breathing quickened. The constant jarring of shields, the soft sand sapping the strength in his legs and the weight of his sword were beginning to take their toll. Once more Hermes advanced; Andax feinted backwards but then, goaded by the crowd, suddenly lunged forward bringing his shield down on his opponent's sword. Hermes swayed back to avoid the scything arc of Andax's sword across his legs. He jumped as he had so many times in training in his youth but the sword just caught his ankle. Domitilla gasped and her hand flew to her mouth. She sensed the Emperor's eyes upon her. Many of the occupants of the imperial box who had been chattering to their neighbours now fell silent and turned to watch the climax. With blood trickling from the wound and sweat pouring down his face Hermes steadied himself. The blow had made him lame. In the centre of the arena he stood like a wounded lion waiting for a pack of hyenas to finish him. His breath was coming more easily yet the damaged ankle made it difficult to turn quickly as the Samnite circled him, looking for the opportunity to strike the fatal blow. The crowd howled encouragement to both. Some supported Hermes whom they remembered in his prime; others wanted to see the new champion crowned. It was clear that Hermes was weakening. Once, wheeling round to face his opponent, he stumbled and Domitilla turned her head away when Andax's sword caught the flange of Hermes's helmet with a heavy clang. Somehow the former champion extricated himself and stood once more unsteadily. Around him the sand was sprinkled with his blood. Limping he dragged himself towards Andax who danced confidently away. The crowd roared on the wounded man. Suddenly the ankle buckled and Hermes was down on one knee with his shield resting on the ground. Andax saw his chance to move in for the kill.

His sword came up to strike while his shield guarded his naked chest. Women screamed and the drums rolled in anticipation of the end. Hermes waited, still resting on one knee. Andax's sword came crashing down. With a desperate effort the old champion thrust up his shield to strike his opponent's forearm with its sharp rim. In the lower tiers the crowd heard the crack of the snapping bone and Andax's sword fell from his shattered grasp. In the same movement Hermes thrust his own sword upwards into the Samnite's exposed belly. For a few seconds the young champion writhed in the sand and then lay still.

Hermes pushed himself to his feet and raised his sword and shield aloft to acknowledge the wild applause of the crowd. Swaying with fatigue he dragged his aching limbs towards the imperial box. His head was stained red where his own helmet had bitten into the flesh under the impact of a blow. One eye was half closed and his left boot was covered with congealed blood. Domitilla longed to take him in her arms, to bathe his wounds and bring this nightmare to an end. Hispo had survived. He would live. Isis had protected him in the struggle against Seth. She felt no sense of triumph, only a swelling in her heart of gladness and gratitude. Domitian watched and leaned towards his dwarf to whisper something in his ear. The ponderous head nodded and then grinned toothlessly at Domitilla who had eyes only for Hispo.

An attendant dressed in black as Charon, the ferryman of departed souls across the river Styx, ran into the arena. He struck Andax on the forehead with his wooden mallet to signify his ownership of the corpse. Mercury, escort of the dead to the underworld, followed. He prodded the lifeless Samnite with a red-hot branding iron to make sure he was not feigning death. Many of the crowd booed and wept as the corpse was impaled on a metal hook and dragged across the sand to the Porta Libitinaria, the exit named after the goddess of burials. The young champion was dead, but 'long live Hermes' shouted others as he stood before the Emperor waiting to receive his prize, a bowl of golden coins and the victor's frond of palm. He had removed his helmet and laid it on the sand beside his sword. He leaned a little on his shield to support his injured foot. His matted hair glistened with sweat when he pushed it back from his eyes with a weary gesture of his hand.

Domitian made no movement from the couch where he had reclined since the beginning of the contest, eating cutlets and asparagus. He flicked his fingers to a soldier of the Praetorian Guard behind the box. A message was despatched to the musicians who raised their trumpets again in a long fanfare. The drums rolled in a crescendo like peeling thunder and the crowd gave a great shout as they recognised the signal for a fresh gladiator. Alemannus, from the forests of Germany, stood for a moment in the shady entrance to the gladiators' gateway and then strode into the sunlight. He was a full six inches taller than any of his rivals in the ring and from his helmet spewed an extravagant plume of egret feathers dyed black, so that he appeared like a giant among his fellows. In his left hand he carried a huge thrusting spear and in his right a long shield on which was emblazoned the face of the Gorgon Medusa with serpents for her hair, long fangs for teeth and a tongue which protruded in a thin red streak.

Hispo knew his fate before he turned. The Emperor had condemned him to fight again immediately. The crowd howled their protests but to no avail. The dwarf grinned and clapped his hands at the approaching Alemannus. Hermes stooped to pick up his arms. He turned to face Domitilla and raised his sword in a salute. She saw his lips move but the words were inaudible in the din. As the German came towards him Hermes replaced his helmet and then limped toward his executioner. Orestilla held a cup of wine sweetened with honey to her mistress's lips. Domitilla took a few sips and closed her eyes. Pain, anger and sorrow wrestled in her head. She saw the contortions on the face of Laocöon and her own face twisted in the suffocation of her love and the return of loneliness. Orestilla stood in front of her until the spectacle in the arena was over.

Hispo had taken the gladiator's oath to fight and, if necessary, to die bravely. Despite his exhaustion he resisted the onslaught of the German for several minutes. He parried and thrust with his sword, even inflicting a flesh wound on his opponent's thigh. Yet he could not match the agility and speed of the fresh man. The long spear of Alemannus soon found its mark and blood spurted from a deep gash in Hermes' own thigh. He went down on both knees unable to support his body any longer. The crowd in unison screamed at the Emperor 'let him live.' Wave after wave of this plea bombarded the ears of Domitilla, hunched and numb now in her seat.

'Why doesn't he raise his finger to ask for mercy? He has fought well and for so long. Surely the Emperor will grant him "missio,"' muttered Julia Frontina to her husband. But Senecio shook his head.

'Hermes is too brave for that. He will never plead with Domitian now.'

The Emperor rose from his couch and stood before his subjects. From his purple toga his right arm shot out. He held it still before him. The shouting of the people died away to silence. All eyes were fixed upon his horizontal thumb. The world stopped and waited on that stubby finger. 'Look,' Domitian shouted, 'he does not ask for mercy because he does not merit it.' He turned his thumb upwards to the sky and his people groaned at the fatal gesture.

On the sand Hermes raised himself onto one knee and clasped his conqueror's thigh as he had been taught to do. The German seized his victim's head and thrust his spear through the neck which Hermes held out to him. He had died like a gladiator should.

CHAPTER IX

APOTHEOSIS

Domitilla stumbled down the steps leading out of the amphitheatre. One or two hands reached out to assist her but she brushed them aside. Orestilla followed, calling out and saying that she would summon the litter. Domitilla pushed her gently away and set off up the hill towards the Golden House. The streets were still empty save for the odd stallholder waiting for the crowds to emerge at the end of the day's show. She lifted the hem of her dress and hurried up the slope into the shade of the colonnade. She leant against one of the columns to catch her breath and fanned her face which was stained with tears and sweat. She realised she had no handkerchief; Orestilla always kept them for her. She wiped her face with the folds of her skirt like some common woman of the street. She smiled ruefully, remembering that it was only prostitutes who were forbidden the use of a litter. She began to walk to the end of the building where Hispo's rooms were. There was nobody to be seen and she found a small wooden door used by slaves as a side entrance. She pressed and it swivelled on its wooden axis. Inside she followed a passage through to a kitchen and up a narrow flight of steps which led to the dark corridor at the back of the palace. Soon she was sitting under the fig tree in the little courtyard behind Hispo's rooms. She drew comfort from the warmth of the afternoon sun and the familiarity of her surroundings. She looked down at the cameo ring and stroked it with her fingers. One or two figs lay on the pavement beneath her feet. She chose a ripe one from the tree and very slowly smeared its contents on her chest and the upper part of her breast not covered by her dress. The sticky seeds adhered to her skin. Her mind grew calmer as she yielded to the still solitude of the place, so that even the occasional roar from the amphitheatre in the valley below did not disturb her.

When she awoke the sun was beginning to set. The courtyard lay in shadow. She walked down the little flight of steps into Hispo's room. The table was bare and everything had been tidied away. Some clothes were neatly folded on a bench and the floor had been freshly swept. She could find no trace of food and the lamps had no oil in them. In the bedroom it was the same. Some blankets had been stacked on top of a cupboard. The bed itself was bare except for his wooden sword which had been laid on it. Domitilla looked round at these simple objects. He must have known that he was going to his death and that they would not meet again. She picked up the sword and carried it back into the room at the front. She propped it up against a chair and knelt down on a little rush mat. She brushed the dried fig seeds from her breast and rubbed them on the wooden blade. She began to pray to Isis and as she did so the hilt of the sword resolved itself into the face of Hispo. The crosspiece became his arms and the blade his body. She heard a voice praying for his soul; the spirit of the goddess had invaded the room through the palest of light cast by her moon which had risen into a sky of faded mauve. Domitilla closed her eyes and pulled the sword towards her, kissing the smooth ash and dampening it with her tears.

Outside Orestilla waited with the litter. The crowds had long since poured out of the amphitheatre and straggled home. Slaves were clearing away the detritus of another day's slaughter and renewing the sand on the floor of the arena. She spotted her mistress emerge from the colonnade, holding the sword with both arms folded across her breast. She hurried over with the bearers, anxious to get Domitilla back to the Palatine before it grew darker. She helped her to climb in and drew the curtains, ordering the bearers to head straight for the palace. But when they reached the Via Sacra, Domitilla dropped her maid at the foot of the path leading up to the palace and instructed the bearers to proceed to the temple of Isis.

Still clutching the sword she walked through the portals of the temple where the precentor came forward to greet her.

'My lady, it is late in the day. We have completed the last service. I'm afraid that the holder of the keys is about to close the doors and I have veiled the statue of the goddess for the night.'

'Pollius, I do not require anything except to pass the night in the cell where I slept before my initiation.'

The precentor looked at her and the sword. 'May I ask why you are carrying that wooden sword. It seems a strange thing to bring into the temple.' He listened gravely to Domitilla's account of the death of Hispo and her prayer to the goddess in his rooms. When she had finished the priest led her to the sanctuary where the mummified effigy of Osiris lay on its bier. 'Tomorrow,' he said, 'we shall make arrangements for the passage of Hispo's soul to the underworld. Now you must lay the sword next to Osiris for safekeeping. In the sword we can preserve his soul in readiness for the journey.'

In the morning, the lady of the sacred procession,

Isiginea, came to Domitilla and took away her dress. Later four young women with stoups of warm water washed her whole body three times to purify it. They clothed her in a robe of deep blue and a pair of gilded sandals. The precentor prayed with her before the image of the goddess, ordering Domitilla on no account to leave the precincts of the temple until the procession started at the setting of the sun.

Slowly the water clock marked the passage of the hours until at last Isiginea came to say that all was ready. At the head of the procession ran small boys, shouting to bystanders, 'Make way, make way. The goddess of the Nile wishes to pass.' Behind followed the women in linen dresses with petals in their hair. Some carried a candle in one hand and a mirror of polished bronze in the other to reflect the light. Young girls scattered on the ground sprigs of lavender and rosemary which gave off a heady scent as their feet crushed them underfoot. The sound of timbrels, reed pipes and flutes came from the musicians who followed in their wake. Four shaven-headed priests from the temple of Serapis carried a small boat of polished citrus wood on their shoulders. Its mast was Hispo's sword bound with linen and a small sail was attached to the blade. On the sail appeared the image of a bird and as they walked Domitilla asked what it meant.

'In the temple at Heliopolis in Egypt are kept the burnt remains of a giant bird which came out of Arabia. They are worshipped as the spirit of Osiris which rises from the ashes to live again.'

Behind Domitilla the precentor walked in front of a seated image of the goddess holding the child Horus in her lap. From her forehead rose an asp cast in silver and her hair was crowned with a bull's horns framing a gilded moon. Her image was escorted by Anubis whose face was painted half white and half black to represent the journey from the world of the living to the world of the dead. On his head he bore the dog's mask which Domitilla recognised from her initiation and the pediment at the entrance to the temple. Last, in single file, the priests walked with the sacred exhibits; the left hand of justice, the palm fronds of gold foil and the sacred jar from which flowed a trickle of milk. The girls danced to the rhythm of the sistrum and sang the lamentation of Isis for her brother/husband; 'Behold, my lord, there is no god to compare with you. I am your protection and our son Horus shall rule the kingdoms of Egypt. Yours is the image of the earth and the heavens reside in your soul. You are dead but will rise again to care for the departed.'

On the banks of the Tiber close to the Fabrician bridge the procession halted. The girls with the candles formed two lines leading down to the water's edge. The lights reflected in the slow dark river blackened by the night sky. The choir fell silent; only the regular beat of the sistrum could be heard as the priests advanced and carefully lowered the boat into the water. One held it still while the precentor purified it with a sprinkling of water from the sacred stoup. Then he placed spices, pomegranate, apples and cow's milk inside the little hull. Isiginea took Domitilla's hand and together they stepped forward. From the priest of the ship Domitilla received an earthenware lamp which she placed in the prow of the boat. The choir began to sing again, chanting their prayers for the safe and speedy journey of the boat and the soul of Hispo. Isiginea gave a sign to the priest of the boat who gently pushed it into the river where for a few moments it swung uncertainly. Then the current caught the stern and it drifted downstream, away into the darkness. Domitilla watched the white mast and sail guided by the flickering lamp until the boat passed under the arches of the bridge and out of sight. She sensed a stirring in the crowd behind her. She turned to look but her arms were seized by strong hands. She found herself confronted by the cuirasses of two praetorian guards and her eyes caught the glint of their drawn swords.

CHAPTER X

DOUBT

In the closed carriage Domitilla had no idea where she was being taken. A surly guard sat beside her. He said nothing throughout the journey and when the carriage came to a halt she was bundled out and down some dark steps into an underground passage lit at intervals by smoky brands. She coughed in the thick fetid atmosphere. Once again she was seized by the arms and propelled along. On each side of her men were standing, clad only in filthy loincloths some of which had slipped down their thighs. She realised that they were chained by heavy metal links round one arm and one leg to rings in the walls. Their unshaven faces were sunk on their chests streaked with sweat and grime; none looked up as she passed. One man appeared to have collapsed altogether and was down on his knees with his chained arm twisted round above his head. The stench of faeces mingled with the sickly odour of tallow in the dirty orange light. They reached a heavy door which one of the guards pushed open. Domitilla found herself in a small cell. At first it was so dark that she could see nothing. She heard the sound of a bolt being shot home and then silence. Looking up she saw a narrow shaft of light coming from a grille high up in one wall. In a corner she made out what at first she took to be a wooden shelf. She felt the top and found it was covered in a thin layer of straw, like bedding for an animal.

Domitilla wondered whether she had been brought to the Tullianum prison near the Forum. But the place seemed too big and besides she sensed that the carriage had borne them away from the centre of the city and towards the outskirts. She sat down on the wooden shelf. Until then she had had no time to think. It had all happened so quickly. She began to feel frightened in the darkness and the silence. She tried to pray to Isis. She remembered that the goddess was the great protectress. But what had she protected? Hispo had been cruelly slaughtered in the arena, murdered by the Emperor. Now she found herself thrown into prison, no doubt to await her own fate at the whim of a mad uncle. Surely Isis should have been able to prevent this. Perhaps she had not prayed hard enough or had displeased the goddess by her actions. It was inevitable that the Emperor would discover her love affair with Hispo. How could she have been so foolish not to realise that? If she had not allowed herself to fall in love with him his corpse would not now be lying in some dusty cart, waiting to be buried in a common grave outside the city or perhaps burnt with executed criminals. Her body convulsed with sobs and she sank back on the straw. Eventually the tears were exhausted and she stared blankly into the semi-darkness, overwhelmed at the horror of what she had done. Her misery gave way to a feeling of bitter resentment. After all, was it so very wrong to fall in love with a man, even if he came from a different class and background? She was being punished for doing something completely natural, by a tyrant who often enough bedded women who were no more than slaves, let alone citizens. But then she remembered she was a priestess of Isis. What had Domitian done with his chief Vestal Virgin when it was discovered that she had broken her vows and had sexual relations with men? Poor Cornelia, buried alive in accordance with the ancient law. Was that what Domitian had in store for her? Would she be bound with a silken rope, then lowered into a sealed cavity and left to die when the air ran out? Perhaps he would keep her here in this cell until thirst and starvation did their work. She noticed there was no water and the warm air had made her thirsty. She got up and banged on the door; nobody came and she could hear nothing. As she went back to the wooden shelf she tripped over something and found it was an empty bucket. She relieved herself in it and lay down on the prickly straw. She fell asleep.

Long before the bolt shot back she had woken. From the dull gleam through the grille above, Domitilla knew it was daylight. She felt a stab of fear as the bolt rattled in the door. Had they come for her? Was it her last day? Could she die bravely as Hispo had? A soldier stepped aside and Domitilla recognised the figure of Norbanus, the Prefect of the Guard. The soldier stood next to him with a drawn sword. For a moment Domitilla thought he had come to run her through there and then. She gave a low moan and cowered against the wall, waiting for the thrust into her guts.

Norbanus spoke. 'All right, Lentulus, I think I can look after myself. Wait outside will you.' The soldier sheathed his sword and withdrew. The Prefect, tall and with the rugged, sunburned face of a Calabrian, surveyed Domitilla briefly. 'I'm sorry to confine you here, but you will appreciate that my orders come from the Emperor.'

Domitilla recovered herself and brushed a few flecks of straw from her dress. To stop her hands shaking she clasped them together. 'May I ask where "here" is and why I am being held in this way?'

'My lady, this is the barracks of the Praetorian Guard near the Porta Nomentana. As to why you have been brought here, I cannot say. Yesterday I received a warrant sealed by the Emperor for your arrest.'

'I don't suppose you know how long I am to be detained or what is to become of me?'

'I'm afraid I cannot guess at the intentions of the Emperor. You know as well as I do that his mood swings from day to day.' Something in his words and expression emboldened Domitilla.

'Is it possible that you might arrange for my freedman Stephanus to visit me? I should like some writing materials and perhaps even some fresh clothes.' Norbanus looked round at the door and saw it was slightly ajar. He walked over to it, said something to the guard and pushed it to.

'My lady, I cannot promise anything. You know that there is no man, even me, who isn't watched day and night.' He paused and then looked up. 'I can perhaps see Stephanus at the palace tonight. That grille is in a wall which forms the perimeter of the barracks. There is no patrol there, but if he is caught placing anything through it, I shan't be able to protect him. The guards will cut him down on the spot.' He turned on his heel, knocked on the door and was gone.

A few minutes later the guard reappeared, this time with an attendant who brought sweet mulled wine on a bronze tray with some bread and honey. Domitilla noticed that the guard kept looking longingly at the tray. She offered him a piece of the bread on which she had spread some of the honey. He was about to take it when the attendant said, 'That's the Prefect's breakfast. He told me it was to be given to this lady.' The soldier hastily withdrew his hand and the door banged behind them.

Domitilla ate and drank quickly, for it was many hours since a handsome Greek boy had served her with roasted thrushes stuffed with almonds before the start of the show in the arena. Then she sat back on the wooden shelf, having first brushed aside the straw to make a space for herself. The wood was hard but the straw looked dirty and she wondered when it had last been changed. She was feeling a little better.

If Stephanus could bring her a stylus and writing block she would write letters to her sons explaining what had happened. But how would the letters ever reach them? She could not place them in the imperial post. She would have to get them to Stephanus who could find a reliable courier. Suppose Stephanus never came. For all she knew, he too might have been arrested, perhaps even executed. Look what had happened one night to poor Epaphroditus, recalled from exile and then mysteriously found dead in a library that he never used. The slight feeling of relief brought about by breakfast and the meeting with Norbanus wore off. Domitilla's thoughts turned back to the terrible scene in the arena. She saw the expression on Hispo's face as he saluted her. She remembered his tears at their last meeting in the Golden House when he had kept from her the knowledge of his fate. Now, at best, she would be condemned to rot in prison for the rest of her life or be killed in some way that she dared not contemplate. It was useless to expect any mercy from Domitian. His treatment of Clemens and Hispo was proof of that.

As she lay on the wooden shelf her depression deepened. There seemed to be no possible end to her misery and loneliness, except a violent death. The comfort and release which the goddess had brought by the spring at Albanum and later in the temple were tinged now with disillusion. Isis had been nothing but a fraud. Her life had lost any sense of purpose or usefulness. Her family had gone; Hispo had been taken from her; it was time to finish with it all. She remembered a wicked old crone who lived somewhere behind the Clivus Opius. Venella, that was her name. She had once heard Julia Procula mention her as being somebody who could prescribe love potions, but Domitilla had been told that she dealt in poisons as well. She would take poison; that would be her escape. Stephanus could push whatever was needed through the grille. She wondered what would be the quickest and least painful. Names skittered through her mind; hemlock, wolfsbane, monkshood. She had no idea how they worked. Stephanus must find out. If only he would come.

She lay in a stupor of unhappiness, in a limbo between sleep and wakefulness. It was impossible even to judge the passing of the hours. It seemed to be just as light outside as when Norbanus had come to see her. She wondered if she could make herself die there and then. She tried to make her heart stop beating by an effort of will. She cried out in frustration at the sheer emptiness around her. Nothing distracted her from her thoughts and her misery.

Once more the bolt shot back and two guards appeared. This time no attempt was made to hide her destination, for the carriage was an open one. With an escort of four horsemen they clattered through the old Servian wall which had guarded republican Rome, over the Quirinal hill and past the gardens of Lucullus. Soon they reached the Clivus Argentarius above which rose the temple of Juno Moneta. To her left the forum of Julius Caesar was crowded with stalls and tradesmen who offered their wares from the porticoes surrounding the square. Sedan chairs and litters threaded their way through the throng. Above it all towered the Corinthian columns of the temple of Venus Genetrix, the goddess whose statue painted in red and gold adorned the cella and from whom the dictator had claimed descent. For a moment Domitilla thought she was being transferred to the Tullianum but the carriage rattled down into the Forum past the arch of Augustus and the House of the Vestals, then up the slope to the entrance to the Domus Augustana, a high archway supported by huge fluted columns of black marble.

Norbanus stepped forward as Domitilla was ordered out of the carriage. Behind him stood two large Germans of the household bodyguard. Dark blue plumes hung from their helmets. Norbanus indicated that Domitilla was to follow him through the wide peristyle which lay behind the archway. She heard the clanking footsteps of the guards behind her as they passed into the rear courtyard where the shallow pool was lined with brilliant white mosaic on which the figures of octopuses, dolphins, crocodiles and sea monsters were picked out in jet and obsidian. She followed Norbanus into the chambers beyond. Clerks were busy at their desks near the wooden niches on the walls which held the records and scrolls. Some looked up and Domitilla sensed their surprise at seeing her go by under armed escort. Nobody was unwise enough to say anything or even to exchange a glance with his neighbour.

At the end of a passage the little party emerged into the sunlight of a curved balcony high above the Great Circus and looking over the Aventine hill. Here they came into the presence of the Emperor. He had his back to them and was examining the birds in a large aviary built into the colonnade which formed a shady release from the glare of the western sun. A slave boy was handing to the Emperor titbits which he tossed through the bars and then watched the birds squabbling for the best morsels. Beside him sat Cocceius Nerva and blind Messallinus with his long cane resting against his chair. At first Domitian either did not hear or affected not to hear the arrival of Norbanus and his prisoner. They stood for some moments in the sun while the Emperor continued to feed his birds. Messallinus, who had certainly detected that somebody was waiting, eventually drew his master's attention to the presence of others on the balcony.

Domitian turned irritably and, noting the figures silhouetted in the glare, told them to step forward under the colonnade so that he could see them properly. He removed his hat carefully to wipe the sweat from his forehead.

'I see,' he said coldly without looking at Domitilla, 'that you have found my niece at last.'

Norbanus betrayed nothing by the expression on his face. 'My lord and god, the lady Domitilla was arrested near the Fabrician bridge. It appears that she was taking part in a procession of worshippers of the goddess Isis and had spent the previous night and day in the temple. That is why we were unable to trace her.'

The Emperor shifted uncomfortably in his seat. He flicked his fingers at a slave who came forward to fan the air which was stifling even in the shade. He sipped from a cup of sherbet while his eyes rested on Domitilla. She dared not speak and kept her own eyes fixed on the marble pavement. Far away below could be heard the occasional shouts of charioteers training their horses in the Great Circus. The twittering of the birds in the aviary emphasised the silence.

Domitian leaned forward and spat out a few words like grape pips. 'I once escaped with my life disguised as an acolyte of the goddess Isis. Did you know that?'

Domitilla realised that he was speaking to her. She looked up and said, 'No, I did not.'

'I was eighteen at the time, fighting with my uncle Sabinus against Vitellius. We were besieged in the Capitol and my uncle was killed the following day.' He paused and then said with a sly grin, 'But I escaped by mingling in an Isaic procession and then I spent the night with Cornelius Primus.'

'What a blessed day that was for Rome!' It was Messallinus who broke in, leering blankly about him.

'I trust you refer to my survival and not to the death of my uncle.'

'My lord and god, of course,' cried Messallinus, twisting his fingers on his cane.

'As I was saying, I have always had a great respect for the worship of the goddess, since that time when we were fighting to win the empire for the Flavians. Indeed, when the temple was burnt down some years ago I paid for its restoration. I don't suppose you knew that either.'

'I was aware that the temple had been restored but not that you had paid for it.'

'Of course not!' Domitian shouted, slapping his hand down on his thigh. 'Throughout my reign I have tried to follow the example set by my glorious predecessor, the divine Augustus, to be the curator of the laws and morals of the Empire. I have worshipped the traditional gods and supported the new religions where they were suitable for our people. Nobody has done more to restore our temples and to encourage citizens in the observance of the rituals handed down to us from our ancestors.'

Domitilla stared in front of her. The Emperor was working himself into an artificial frenzy, jabbing his finger in the air. He paused and mopped his brow with a handkerchief. Nobody moved.

'But you,' he clenched the handkerchief in his fist, 'have seen fit to defile the house of the Flavians and the priesthood of Isis. Do you realise how you have insulted the imperial family by running about with this gladiator? You have behaved no better than a common slut. You! The granddaughter and twice niece of emperors of Rome. It was bad enough when Eppia eloped with Sergiolus. At least she was only the daughter of a senator. I suppose you were attracted by Hispo's good looks. He's not so pretty now.'

Domitilla made no answer.

'Well, I'll say this for you, you had better taste than Eppia. Your gladiator didn't have an enormous wart on his nose and a permanently runny eye.' He held out his cup and a slave hastened forward to refill it.

'You know how I deal with priestesses who have sex, I presume?'

Domitilla looked up into the face of the man who had put away her husband, the father of her children for all his worthlessness, and Hispo whom she had loved. He could dispose of her too with as little compunction as the flies impaled on his stylus. This was not a human being but an egocentric monster in whose tiny brown eyes she detected the shadow of fear and guilt. The futility of her position lent her courage of which she had not thought herself capable.

'I take it that you are referring to the burial alive of Cornelia. I am not aware that any vow of chastity binds the priestesses of Isis or that I have infringed any law by my relationship with Hispo. If I have brought dishonour to the house of the Flavians then I regret it. I am already resolved to take poison to put an end to my life even if you were to see fit to spare it. But my death will not be out of a sense of shame; it will be because I have brought about the death of a man I loved.'

Domitian contemplated her for a moment. 'Oh no. You are not going to get off that easily. In your case I have decided to revive a tradition of the Julio-Claudians when they had to deal with an evil and immoral woman. The divine Augustus was the first to make use of it when he discovered that his daughter Julia was a sheath for every loose blade in Rome. Then Tiberius had to send Julia's daughter Agrippina on the same trip to stop her mischief-making tongue, and dear old Nero packed Octavia off there on a charge of adultery, though the evidence was a bit thin in her case.' He laughed and both Nerva and Messallinus quickly joined in. But Domitian stopped them. 'Do you know where I mean?'

'I think you mean exile on an island off the coast of Campania. I do not know its name.'

'Pandataria! You won't take long to get to know it. They say you can walk round it easily enough in a couple of hours. You'll stay on that island until you die. My staff there are very efficient. They won't let you kill yourself. Take her away, Norbanus, and see that she is conveyed by boat from Misenum without delay.'

Norbanus nodded and motioned to the guards. As they walked back through the palace, Stephanus, who had heard of his mistress's arrival, came hurriedly to greet her but stopped short at the sight of her escort. Norbanus, however, allowed them to speak briefly and Domitilla gave him a message for her sons so they would at least know their mother's fate.

That night as she sat on the shelf in the darkness she heard a thud on the floor of the cell. Somebody had dropped a roll of papyrus through the grille. In the morning she untied it and read, 'Stay alive! Pray to the goddess. She is your protectress and redeemer. Do not doubt her.'

A few days later Domitilla reached Misenum and was escorted aboard the ship to take her into exile. She remembered the prophesy of the old man in the temple: that she would make a journey by sea.

CHAPTER XI

RETRIBUTION

In his dream the Emperor saw Minerva, the spear in her hand broken, riding a silver chariot drawn by four black horses. The chariot flew below dark scudding clouds through which lightning flashed. Minerva was screaming that Jupiter had disarmed her. Her cheeks streamed with tears and her face was contorted with terror. Suddenly the chariot tumbled over a precipice into a gaping black hole and was gone.

Claps of thunder echoed over the city and shafts of lightning lit up momentarily the basilicas and monuments around the palace and the forums. Jupiter himself was raining thunderbolts down upon Rome from the heights of his temple on the Capitoline where the white marble columns of its portico stood like giants against the tortured sky. Domitian awoke with a start as the building shook under another explosion of noise. He was sweating profusely and threw off the covers though the night was not particularly warm. He called for Parthenius who slept in a cubicle off the Emperor's bedchamber. The latter was already awake and came through with a lamp and a towel to dry his master's face and chest.

'I dreamt that Jupiter had defiled Minerva and then driven her to her death. She cannot protect me now.' His hand shook as he reached for the goblet of wine on the table beside his bed.

'My lord god, it is only a thunderstorm; listen, it is moving away. Tomorrow will be bright and fine. You have nothing to fear from Jupiter; after all you are a god like him.'

'Don't be a fool!' Domitian hurled his goblet against the wall. 'Can't you see that I am surrounded by men and gods who desire my death? But I'll beat them.' He was breathing heavily and sitting on the edge of the bed. 'Caligula punished Neptune, didn't he?'

'My lord god, I believe that he did by striking the sea with his sword and making the legionaries gather the shells on the shore in their helmets.'

'Exactly. The shells are still down in the cellars somewhere.' Domitian began to stride about the room. Then, in a fit of temper, he wrenched the aegis of Minerva from his neck and stamped on it. It lay, unbroken, on the floor. He walked over to the statue of the goddess and with a swipe of his arm sent it crashing to the ground where it cracked in two pieces.

'My lord and god, is this wise?' Parthenius picked up the aegis and placed it on the table.

'She's no use to me now. She's dead, driven to suicide by Jupiter.' Domitian gave a low moan and sank to his knees by the shattered statue. He began to sob, pressing together the two halves of the goddess's head, but they fell apart again. Parthenius led him back to the bed where he slept fitfully until the third hour.

Parthenius was right, for the sun was shining brightly when Euphemus brought in a dish of larks' tongues and some fresh bread.

' My lord god, the Prefect of the Watchmen is outside. He wishes to make his report on the damage caused by the storm last night.'

'Damage? You see that statue there, Euphemus. A clap of

thunder shook this room so hard that it toppled over. Get hold of the best sculptor in Rome. I want a replacement before dusk tonight. Send in Vinicianus.'

The Prefect of the Watchmen, Julius Vinicianus, brought with him a list of major buildings which had suffered some disfigurement in the storm.

'Nothing I think, my lord and god, which will impose a great burden upon the treasury.'

'There'd better not be, after the millions of gold pieces I've spent restoring our temples and arches. Do you not agree, Vinicianus, that the city has never looked more magnificent?'

'My lord and god, Augustus himself would have been jealous of your work. I certainly hear praises as I go about the regions, from senators to the common people, for the beauty which they see all around them.'

'Indeed, the people have much to be thankful for, though I see little evidence of it in their demeanour. So, tell me the worst of the damage.'

'My lord and god, the worst is in the eighth region where the roofs of the warehouses which Agrippa built caught fire and some grain has been lost. The rain soon doused the flames, but some rafters have been burnt.'

'Is there any damage to temples dedicated to the imperial cult?'

Vinicianus consulted his list. 'My lord god, one of the elephants in front of the temple of Fortune in the Field of Mars was struck and its trunk has been shattered. After your triumphant campaign in Sarmatia the people will rejoice that the damage is so trivial.'

'Yes, yes! Anything else?'

Vinicianus hastily looked through his notes again.

'My lord, there was some damage to buildings on the

Quirinal. I believe that a finial fell from the pediment of the temple to your illustrious family and was shattered when it hit the ground. I'm sure it can be replaced.'

'Did you hear that, Parthenius? Now he strikes directly at me. I don't suppose there was any damage to the temple of Capitoline Jupiter?'

'My lord and god, I have no record of anything there.'

'Have some of the gilded tiles dislodged from the roof. Make sure it's done at night so the people don't see. You can replace them in a few days' time. Jupiter's not going to get away with this.'

When Vinicianus had left Domitian sat morosely in a chair looking out into the courtyard. Eventually he spoke. 'You realise what this means, Parthenius?'

'My lord god?'

'These are omens of my death. First I dream about the temple to my family being struck by lightning and then it happens. Now Minerva has abandoned me and her statue has shattered.'

'My lord, a mere finial falling from the roof of a temple is no great matter. It represents the snapping of a tiny twig from the great tree of the Flavian family. The finial is the figure of Domitilla who has disgraced your whole dynasty and whom you have so justly punished. The gods have shattered her in recognition of your pious act in banishing her to restore the purity of your house.'

Domitian brightened. 'Perhaps you're right.' But then he sank back again in the chair. The stylus which he habitually carried twisted in his fingers. 'The Sybil at Cumae was useless. She spoke in rhyming riddles, surrounded by all that green smoke which made me cough. I think she's no more than a witch. I should have had her burnt or thrown into the sea. The only reason I didn't was that my father believed in her.'

'My lord, there is a Chaldaean in the city at the moment. They say his prophecies never lie. I'm sure he would reassure you if you consulted him.'

★ ★ ★

Ascletarion entered the vast reception hall of the Domus Flavia lined with fluted pilasters of pink marble between which he glimpsed statues of emperors and generals decorated each day with wreaths of fresh laurel. The high vault of the gilded roof shone like the sun and beneath his feet lay a sea of green mosaic on which triremes and quinqueremes floated. He was taken through a vestibule which led to a small chamber where Ascletarion came face to face with the Emperor of Rome seated by himself on a chair of cedar wood inlaid with silver. He felt a nudge in his back and, taking the hint, the astrologer prostrated himself on the floor to reveal his brown cloak woven with moons and stars. The two guards raised their right arms in salute and retired to the door which they closed behind them.

'Get up, get up, man. I've no wish to see your back. I can't learn anything about my future from that.'

Ascletarion picked himself up. In his right hand he held the astrologer's staff round which a snake was entwined to represent the twists and sinuosities of time, the governor of all things. His face was dominated by a large hooked nose and from his chin dangled a straggly beard of gingery brown flecked with grey. His bald head was mottled with brown patches where the sun had shrivelled the skin. In the pockets of his cloak he carried the charts, rulers and compasses of his trade.

'Are you the man they call Ascletarion?' The old man, a little breathless after his climb up the hill, nodded. 'Where do you come from and why should I believe anything you say?'

The astrologer gathered himself and looked up for the first time. 'My lord god, I was born on the banks of the Euphrates in the Kingdom of Commagene. When I was a young man I travelled to Alexandria where I studied the works of Thrasyllus. My lord, you will recall that he was the astrologer upon whom the noble Tiberius placed so much reliance. My tutor was Balbillus, son of Thrasyllus and it was he who advised the mighty Nero.'

'That didn't do him much good. Your tutor didn't predict the great fire in the city; Nero told me as much.'

'My lord god, I should have welcomed the opportunity to advise him.'

'What's that stick in your hand? It's not a dagger is it?'

'My lord, it is the wand of time upon which everything depends. It sets us ineluctably upon our course through life as defined by the position of Saturn on the date of our birth. Nothing can change our fate thereafter. You have heard of the poet Manlius, my lord? He wrote at the time of the divine Augustus.'

'I know his work well; indeed I have read it aloud in public. What lines are you referring to?'

'Manlius wrote, "Fate rules the earth and all things stand firm by a fixed law... the moment of our birth also witnesses our death, and our end depends upon our beginning."'

'The worshippers of the goddess Isis would not agree with that. They believe that she has the power to change fate. What do you say to that?'

'My lord, the stars govern our future. Whatever we do, it cannot change.'

'Cicero said that to believe in the inevitability of fate was to ignore the power of cause and effect. He thought that fate was the result of a chain reaction of causes and events which man might influence for good or ill.'

'But my lord, the causes, events and the interference of men are themselves written in the stars.'

'So, it doesn't matter how I behave, well or badly; my fate will be the same for I have no control over the end result.'

'My lord, perhaps there we are confusing the concept of free will with fate. Fate does not deprive a man of the choice between good and evil. It merely defines his end.'

'Enough of this trite learning. I want information about my future. What do you need to know from me?'

'My lord, before I can cast your horoscope I shall need the date upon which the gods were pleased to deliver you to us.'

'I was born on the twenty-fourth day of Domitianus in the eight hundred and twenty-seventh year after the first Olympiad. You know of course that Domitianus is the name by which we now refer to the month of October?'

'So, my lord and god, you were conceived under the sign of Aquarius. If you will give me a few minutes I must make some calculations.'

Ascletarion knelt down and pulled out of his pockets a large chart which he spread on the marble floor. With the aid of a pair of compasses he drew a number of arcs and tangents which intersected with a circle based on the zone of Aquarius. Symbols and signs in Aramaic covered the chart. He began to measure with a ruler and a stylus certain distances between the sun, the moon and the planets. He consulted a table of figures down the side of the chart which was lined on each side with wooden batons of ash.

'Well, what do you see?'

Ascletarion tugged nervously at his lip with his forefinger and thumb. His head began to shake. The stylus slipped from his fingers and rolled across the pavement. He opened his mouth to speak but no words emerged. He knelt helplessly silent as his left hand described a circular movement repeatedly over one zone of the chart. Domitian leapt angrily to his feet and strode over to the kneeling figure. He yanked him upright by his beard and then grabbed his shoulders.

'I asked what you see. May the gods curse you!' he shouted, shaking the old man so that his head jerked backwards and forwards.

'My lord and god,' Ascletarion's teeth were chattering with fear, 'the signs are not good.' He wiped his hand across his mouth. The fingers were bent and wrinkled like the talons of a chicken. 'I see a giant oak tree falling with a crash that shakes the world.'

'An oak tree? Where is this oak tree? You tell me that.' Domitian's fingers bit into the old man's shoulders.

'My lord god, it is not far from Rome, not far.'

Domitian pushed Ascletarion away so that he staggered back and nearly fell. 'On my family's estate near Reate there is an ancient oak tree sacred to the god Mars. Do you mean that tree?'

'My lord god, I cannot be sure of that. I can only read what the stars foretell.'

Both men stood silently. Ascletarion braced himself for another blow but the Emperor's face assumed a calmer expression as he thought for a few moments.

'So, when do you say that this oak tree will fall with such a great crash?'

'It will fall, my lord, at the fifth hour, within thirty days of today.'

Domitian paced up and down between his chair and the chart lying on the pavement. He gazed down at it and then gave it a kick before turning away, not understanding the meaning of the signs and geometric figures. At last he looked up slyly at Ascletarion.

'You say that you never lie. That's right, isn't it?'

'My lord and god, I am an astrologer. I tell what I see in the horoscope. That never lies.'

'Well then, I suppose that you can predict the circumstances of your own death?'

'My lord, I was born in very humble surroundings. My father and mother had no knowledge of the importance of these matters and no record was made of the date of my birth.' Ascletarion hesitated before continuing. 'I had a dream once that I would be set upon by a pack of dogs and torn to pieces and that would be my end. The charts confirm this, but when it will happen, I cannot predict.'

Domitian grunted and resumed his pacing of the room. He went round to stand behind the astrologer. 'Suppose that what you are telling me about the tree is true and it refers to the downfall of the Flavian dynasty. Is there nothing I can do to bend fate a little, some propitiatory act that I could perform?'

'My lord god, if you will allow me to consult the chart again?'

'Yes, yes, go on.'

Ascletarion almost fell to the floor and crawled to fetch his stylus before bending again over the scroll of papyrus. 'I cannot vouch for its effectiveness but there is a school of thought at Rhodes, my lord, which allows that fate can be diverted if one can only discover the correct procedure.'

'Well, you'd better find it,' hissed the Emperor, returning to his chair. Once more the old man peered at the signs and hieroglyphs. His beard brushed over the chart and he held it up with his left hand so that he could see the different divisions of the zodiac.

'Well?' The Emperor was growing impatient again.

Ascletarion pushed himself upright with the aid of his wand. 'I believe there is one way for you to forestall your fate, my lord. You must shave your head under the sign of Aquarius.'

Domitian screamed and hurled his wig at the unfortunate astrologer. It hit Ascletarion on the shoulder and fell to the ground. 'How can I do that you old fool when I'm bald already? Guards!' The doors swung open and two big Germans rushed in. 'This wretch says he always speaks the truth. He predicts my death in thirty days. Very well, I'll prove he is a liar. Take him away and lash him to a wooden pyre. Burn him to a cinder.'

Ascletarion collapsed to the floor with a shriek. The Germans seized him and dragged him from the chamber. Off the Via Appia the guards had soon built a pyre of wood to which Ascletarion was bound hand and foot. The soldiers set a torch to the pyre but as they did so a dark cloud settled overhead and it began to rain heavily, extinguishing the flames.

In the night a pack of dogs came scavenging. They pulled the astrologer from the pyre. At dawn when the guards returned only a few bones remained.

★ ★ ★

Having received the password for the following day from the Emperor and issued it to the officer in command of the palace guard, Norbanus walked back through the outer peristyle of the Domus Augustana towards the pillared gateway. He heard his name called softly and turned to see the Empress, Domitia Longina, standing by herself in the shadows of the colonnade. She beckoned him to a chamber used as a private reception room by the imperial family. Norbanus wondered whether this was some little stratagem by the Empress to get them alone together. For some time he had been aware that Domitia was paying more attention to him than was required by court etiquette. He had been careful not to respond, aware that many pairs of eyes would be watching and that any sign of intimacy would quickly reach the ears of the Emperor. However the peristyle was deserted and he followed the Empress into the room where she had already taken a seat on a dais. He stood before her, waiting respectfully. The Empress looked back at him in silence. To his surprise she did not smile and he realised that she was trembling.

After a few moments she blurted out, 'I have to trust you, Norbanus.' There was a hint of pleading in her voice. He looked steadily at the Empress, wondering what was expected of him.

'Well?'

'My lady, I am a soldier in the service of the Emperor and his family. I hope my loyalty is not in question.'

'No, no, of course not.' Domitia gazed at him again, seemingly unable to make up her mind. At last she drew from the fold of her gown two sheets of paper and held them out. Norbanus stepped forward and took them. He saw that each sheet contained two lists of letters. He recognised the handwriting of the Empress herself. Otherwise they meant nothing to him.

'One of the slave boys found a two-leafed tablet of linden wood in a cupboard in the Emperor's suite yesterday. I caught him looking at it and made a copy. That's the copy.'

Norbanus looked up, his face expressionless. 'My lady, I can make no sense of it. Is it something I should know about?'

'I'm not sure.' The Empress hesitated. 'I think it may be a list of names, in some sort of simple code. The original is in the Emperor's own hand, of course.'

Norbanus looked again at the sheets, but said nothing.

'I think it's a list of victims, or potential victims.'

The last phrase came out as a strangulated sob and she buried her face in her hands before looking up again. 'There are a lot of frightened people in this palace. We don't know where he will strike next. I wondered if you might be of help.' She spread her hands in a little gesture and then nervously adjusted the ringlets of hair by her ears.

'What makes you think it is a list of victims?'

'Once when he was drunk a few months ago I heard him whisper it to Messallinus. He said something like, "He's on my list. It won't be long before Charon's rowing him across." Do you see how some of the sets of letters have been struck through?'

'Who else knows about this?'

'Nobody. I told the slave to put the tablet back where he had found it. He won't say anything. I'm going to my villa at Praeneste tomorrow. I'll take the boy with me and keep him there.'

Two hours later Norbanus was reclining on a couch in the officers' mess of the Praetorian Guard. In front of him lay a half finished pie of hare garnished with watercress and a pitcher of Vesuvium, not so easy to obtain since the eruption had destroyed most of the vines on the slopes of the volcano. It was late in the evening and Norbanus had dined alone. He poured himself another goblet of wine and began to study the two pieces of paper. Supposing the Empress was right and the lists were indeed the disguised names of victims. Somebody had told him once that Caligula had kept a similar record of the names of rich citizens who had been told to alter their wills in the Emperor's favour. When he was short of funds he would consult the list and order one or more names on it to commit suicide.

For a long time Norbanus could make no sense of the

letters. They were not the initials of men who had been executed or exiled. But at length he broke through. It was the letters O.F.T. which gave him the clue. He mouthed them out loud to himself and tried to construct names: Otho, Octavius, Orosius, Ofonius, Orfitus. It struck him that O F and T were the first, third and fifth letters of Orfitus or the Orfiti, a prominent family one of whose members had been elevated to the consulship by Domitian but subsequently executed. Norbanus tried applying the same principle to the other sets of letters and found that he could produce names of men who had been killed, forced to commit suicide or exiled. The rule did not always work until he realised that in some cases the Emperor had not simply used a man's clan name but had taken the first letter of his praenomen, the second letter of his clan name and the third letter of his cognomen to produce a set of three letters. Thus Salvius Otho Cocceianus, who had been executed for celebrating the birthday of his uncle, the Emperor Otho, appeared as S.T.C. on the list. Methodically Norbanus worked through each of the sets of letters until he had identified them all. One or two were designated by a single letter and he could only guess at the person referred to. Wherever the victim was already dead or exiled he noted that the letters had been struck through. His finger came to rest on the letters N.R.A. towards the end of the second page. There was no line through them. Norbanus knew instantly that the letters referred to him. Had the Emperor noticed something in the behaviour of his wife that marked him out for death? He would not be the first. The actor Paris had been struck down in the street for some alleged affair with the Empress.

Norbanus became angry, very angry indeed. He sat quite still, staring in front of him, his hand clasped round the goblet. He looked round at the groups of empty couches used by mean little time-servers, men who had done nothing. How many of them had heard the hiss of a catapult fired in action, had seen a spear juddering in the woodwork of a palisade a hand's breadth from their face or found their comrades nailed to the ground with their legs broken in some German forest? He doubted that some knew how to use the sword that hung at their belt. Yet these parade ground soldiers were paid more than the legionaries who protected the boundaries of the Empire. Since he had been Prefect he had pulled the standard up, but nothing could take the place of active service against the enemy. His officers and tribunes might respect him, yet secretly they laughed behind his back at his country accent. He knew that.

And now this miserable piece of paper. Was this his reward for nearly thirty years of loyal service to the Empire? Was he to be discarded, thrown to the dogs by the Emperor, like an apple core at the end of his meal? Perhaps he would be dragged out by the very guards he commanded, executed and his body exposed like some common criminal. Then Norbanus wondered whether there was a trap. Was Domitia Longina the witting or unwitting agent of a conspiracy in the palace? Was it intended that he, Norbanus, should be deceived into committing some act of treason and thus give the Emperor an excuse for disposing of him? He dismissed this suspicion. Domitian had no need of excuses if his mind was set on murder. And Domitia herself had no reason to love her husband any longer. Had the Emperor not seduced her from her first husband, Aelianus, and executed him because he joked with Titus that he had an excellent singing voice as a result of being forced to abstain from sex? In any case, Domitian engaged in open infidelity with any woman who caught his fancy. The Empress could hardly be blamed if she hated him now.

Perhaps he should consult Tiberius, his co-Prefect of the Guard. Then Norbanus remembered that Tiberius was away from Rome for a few days on his estate at Cosa where Rabirius, the Emperor's architect, was helping him to draw up plans for an extension to his villa. In any case could he trust Tiberius? Suppose he were to betray Norbanus; it would be tempting to take advantage and try to secure the Prefecture for himself alone. He thought of his former commander, Lappius Maximus, Chief Pontiff now. He had always had a soft spot for Norbanus whom he saw as a soldier of the old school. But these days Lappius was very thick with Domitian. Norbanus was shrewd enough to realise that his old general had too much to lose to risk becoming involved. That left the one man upon whom he could rely, himself.

He stood up and went to his office. His sword and belt were lying on the table where he would normally have left them in readiness for the morning. He strapped them on and walked out through the main gates of the barracks. The sentries came to attention and saluted. As he passed the brazier at the gate he dropped in the two pieces of paper and watched them burn. With two torch bearers walking before him he made his way to his house in the street of the amber polishers.

★ ★ ★

The sun was low over the Janiculum hill when Stephanus walked down the steps leading from the old palace of the Emperor Tiberius into the Forum. He passed the house of the Vestals where the six priestesses were chanting their evening hymn, praying for the safety of the city. In the temple itself the sacred flame burned as it had done since the time of King Numa. Beside him rose the great arch of Augustus with its carved reliefs showing the battles of Philippi and Actium. On top rode the Emperor in a triumphal chariot wearing a wreath of laurel and bearing a sceptre crowned with an eagle in his right hand which he extended in a protective gesture across the city of Rome. On the steps of the Julian Basilica a couple of old men were still bent over a game of chequers and a few stalls selling food were open on the other side of the Forum under the arches of the Aemilian Basilica. Most people had gone home, for no business could be transacted after sundown. Before turning right into the Forum Transitorium Stephanus glanced behind him. Nobody appeared to be following and he walked into the centre of the square to the temple of Four-Faced Janus, so called because each of its four doors looked out onto a forum; of Rome, of Augustus, of Peace and the Transitorium itself.

As instructed he waited by the entrance facing the Forum of Peace. He noticed that a flock of ravens had settled on the roof of the temple of Mars and were cawing mournfully in the evening light. One or two others in the square were looking up at the birds, wondering what their meaning might be. Stephanus felt a tap on his shoulder. A man in a cloak was standing next to him.

'You are Stephanus, freedman of Flavia Domitilla?' The man's voice was gruff but not unfriendly. Stephanus thought he detected a sword beneath the cloak and wondered whether he might be a soldier. He stood stiffly as he spoke. 'Follow these instructions, please; walk up the Argiletum and turn right when you reach the Vicus Sandaliarius. About half way along, before the junction with the Clivus Opius, there is an alleyway to the left. On the corner stands a house with large double doors of bronze and above the lintel there is a statue of the god Silvanus carrying a branch in his hand. The right hand door will be barred but the left will swivel on its pivot. Go in and walk down the passage to the room at the end. Wait there.'

Stephanus did as he was bid. He realised that the man in the cloak was following him at a distance. When he reached the bronze doors the one to the left opened and he found himself in a dark passage. As he walked down it he heard a bolt slide behind him. He entered a room decorated with frescoes of the scenes of battles. At one end stood a table laid with fruit and sweetmeats, two silver goblets and a jug of wine. The furnishings were completed by two couches and an elaborate bronze stand of four elephants from whose curved trunks hung oil lamps.

After a few moments Norbanus entered the room through a door opposite the passage. The Prefect of the Guard and the freedman talked late into the night. It was not until dawn the next day that Stephanus returned to the palace.

About a week later it was given out that Stephanus had scalded his left arm in an accident with some hot water. He began to wear a heavy bandage to protect it.

★ ★ ★

It is the eighteenth day of Germanicus, formerly known as September. The sun has not yet risen and the palace sleeps. Two German bodyguards lean idly against the wall near the door which blocks the entrance to a narrow flight of steps. These steps lead from the upper level of the Domus Augustana to the suite of rooms occupied by the Emperor at ground level. Two more sets of stairs give access to the court in front of the Emperor's apartments. One climbs up to the terrace looking out over the Circus Maximus and the other links the court with the stadium where the Emperor may take his exercise unseen by the outside world. Since the prediction of Ascletarion thirty days ago both these staircases have remained unused, locked and bolted. Nevertheless, at the head of each a burly German stands guard. Outside the main gates to the palace, their breath visible in the chill air, a detachment of praetorians in civilian dress but wearing their swords keeps watch. On the order of the Emperor, Norbanus has doubled the number and from time to time pairs of soldiers pace their beat between one guardhouse and the next. Summer lightning flashes over the city, so that for a moment the pale marble walls of the palace and the giant amphitheatre stand out against the dark sky like the snowy mountains of the Alps.

In the shadows of the stadium a figure moves softly along the gravel path before climbing swiftly over the little hedge of box into the bushes near the gilded statue of Hercules. Down on his knees he palms away the soil with his hands to expose a wooden trapdoor ribbed with strong bars of iron. Gently he lifts the door and works the hinges until he is satisfied that it opens easily. He replaces it and brushes over it a thin layer of soil. Soon he is back inside the building carrying clean clothes ready for the new day. His name is Satur and he assists Parthenius in his duties.

On the other side of the city some guards are being turned out early at the praetorians' barracks. Two hundred men from the seventh cohort parade bleary-eyed before the Prefect. They know him well from the time when he was their tribune. This dawn parade is most unusual but the rankers know better than to question Norbanus. He swings up into the saddle of his horse and orders the men to follow him in silence across the city. It is the first hour of the day. Early risers stand aside and watch curiously as the soldiers march past the little taverns and food stalls from which the smells of cooking sausage and fresh bread emerge. Slave boys run with steaming trays of food to the bigger houses and dogs bark as they dispute some fallen scrap.

In the palace Parthenius goes quietly about his tasks. He is a man of slight build, courteous and reserved. He has been in the service of the Emperor for many years, the only man permitted to enter the imperial suite without being searched for weapons. Once Domitian made him swear four times in front of the statue of Minerva that he, Parthenius, would never strike a blow against his master. He hears the Emperor call and enters the bedroom.

'What hour is it, Parthenius? Are we past the dangerous time?'

'My lord and god, it is half way through the third hour. Do you wish to take breakfast now or will you go to the bath first? Veiento has sent you a present of some fine apples.'

'You know perfectly well that I never eat apples in the morning. Save them for tomorrow when I shall be celebrating.'

'Celebrating, my lord?'

'Yes, of course. Don't you realise that tomorrow I shall have proved that scoundrel Ascletarion to be a liar. I shall have survived the thirty days. So much for his stars and charts. I'll go to my bath now and eat afterwards.'

Domitian strode from the room down the passage to the vaulted chamber where Sigerius had prepared the bath. Parthenius sent the altar boy up to the kitchens to order the Emperor's breakfast. Then he moved quickly to the bed and felt under the Emperor's pillow. As he knew he would he found the dagger which Domitian kept there. The weapon shook in his hand. He was not used to handling such things. He wrapped it in a soiled tunic, walked into the passage leading to the courtyard and slipped the weapon into one of the wooden cases in which the Emperor's private scrolls were kept on top of a cupboard. He carried on into the courtyard where one of his own freedmen, Maximus, and Satur were waiting. He beckoned them to follow him back to the antechamber where the Emperor kept his day couch. While Parthenius watched the other passage in case Domitian should return early from the bath, the two men slid through the trapdoor in the floor of the antechamber down into the tunnel leading to the stadium and the trapdoor at the other end. Two years before Domitian had ordered the construction of the tunnel to provide a means of escape if his apartment were surrounded by assassins. There Maximus and Satur waited in the dark and the damp. The gold pieces would reward this temporary discomfort.

Norbanus supervised the changing of the guard at the palace gates. Better to have men of the seventh cohort on hand whom he knew would obey his orders. He sent the detachment from the second cohort back to the barracks. They were pleased to be relieved of their duties so unexpectedly early in the day. He passed the water clock in the inner peristyle. It showed that the fourth hour had nearly drained away.

Domitian lay on his day couch. The sun was warm and he sank back, gazing at the ceiling. Outside in the court he could hear the trickle of the fountain. Somewhere inside, the altar boy and Parthenius were preparing his ceremonial toga for the following day. Yes, he would make a visit to the Senate and read to them the poem he was composing. It need not be long but would celebrate his survival of the evil prophecies of his death. He scratched with his stylus on the paper. He felt a little sleepy. The paper dropped from his hand and he dozed for a moment.

Stephanus was a powerfully built man, not yet thirty years of age. He had served his mistress Domitilla since he was ten when Clemens's agent had bought a batch of slaves including him and his father at the slave market on Delos. One day when Domitilla's sons were small they had been receiving riding lessons on the family estate near Reate. The horse on which young Vespasianus was mounted had suddenly bolted. It was found afterwards to have been stung near the eye by a bee. At the time Stephanus was holding the bridle. He was only thirteen years old. Hanging on the horse's neck he had gradually brought it to a halt and returned Vespasianus safe and sound. On another occasion on the road to Tibur when Domitilla had been travelling in a small open carriage drawn by two horses with Stephanus riding as postilion they had been set upon by four brigands. Stephanus had wielded a stave with such ferocity that the thieves had fled empty handed and much bruised. So well was he regarded that he had gained his manumission much sooner than most slaves who could normally expect to receive their freedom only on the death of their master, if at all. Now Domitilla was banished to some remote island and resentment at her treatment burned deep in her former servant who had always loved her from a distance.

He walked along the passages and through the great courts of the palace. His left arm was swathed in the bandage which he had lately assumed. At the head of the steps leading down to the imperial apartments the two Germans still lolled. There was little to occupy their time. In the previous month few persons other than the Emperor's body servants had approached this part of the palace. The Germans saw Stephanus coming. His uniform told them that he was an attendant of some kind, a person to whom they could be insolent.

'And what might you be wanting, my lad?' a studied

piece of rudery considering that Stephanus was older than the guard who spoke to him, though not as tall.

'I have important information which concerns the safety of the Emperor and not you,' replied Stephanus stiffly. 'Kindly arrange for me to be conducted to him. The head chamberlain will vouch for my identity. I am Stephanus, freedman of the lady Domitilla.'

'We don't care who you are matey. You're not going past us, not even if you are the Emperor's Greek bum boy.'

'Very well. I shall have to summon the Prefect of the Guard. I'm sure he'll be able to teach you some manners. You may not be aware that he is here in the palace early today.' The remark went home. The Germans looked at each other and surveyed Stephanus with a slightly more respectful air.

'You'll have to be searched,' said one of them. 'Can't go through the door otherwise.' He began to pat Stephanus about the body. It was soon apparent that he carried no weapon. 'What's that bandage? Take it off.' Stephanus slowly unwound the cloth. Underneath was revealed an area of bruising and swelling where Stephanus had flicked the bicep with a wet towel and rubbed in some vinegar. When the guard touched it, he winced. 'Go and fetch the chamberlain. See if he knows this bloke.'

While they waited for the other guard to return Stephanus wrapped the bandage carefully round his arm again. He heard footsteps in the passage behind him and wondered whether somebody else was on his way to call upon the Emperor. But whoever it was turned away and Stephanus listened with relief to the sound of retreating footsteps somewhere on the marble pavement above. At last the guard came back up the staircase accompanied by Parthenius.

'This man says he has business with the Emperor,' said the senior guard, addressing Parthenius. 'Do you suppose the

Emperor wishes to see him? I've searched him. He's not carrying anything.'

Parthenius looked steadily at Stephanus. 'May I know the nature of the business? The Emperor is occupied at the moment and would only wish to be disturbed if the matter were important.'

'It concerns the safety of the state, and more importantly the safety of the Emperor's person. I have information about a possible conspiracy.'

'Very well. If you wait here I will ask the Emperor whether he wishes to see you.' Parthenius disappeared down the steps and once again Stephanus waited. The guards had lost interest in him and began discussing some bet on a chariot race in which Incitatus was to ride for the purples that afternoon. Up above in the peristyle the water clock indicated the approach of the fifth hour.

Parthenius found his master seated at the table in the antechamber, scribbling furiously. 'I've nearly finished it,' he cried triumphantly, holding up the scroll for Parthenius to see. 'A little polishing this afternoon and I'll have it done. We must send a message to the consuls instructing them to convene the Senate tomorrow. I want them to hear this. It will do them good. Then they can pass a decree banishing all astrologers from the city in gratitude for my survival.'

'My lord and god, the freedman Stephanus is here to see you. He says he has information concerning the safety of the state and possibly a conspiracy against yourself.' The cheerfulness of the moment disappeared from Domitian's face. The small brown eyes assumed their habitual hostile, yet fearful expression.

'Is he by himself?'

'My lord, he is. I don't think you have anything to fear from him. The guards have searched him. He seems anxious to convey his information to you.'

'What hour is it?' asked Domitian sharply.

'My lord and god, it is past the sixth hour,' said Parthenius, conscious that the sun was in the wrong position in the sky. The Emperor could not see it from where he sat.

'It's a little warm in here. I'll see him in my bedchamber.'

Parthenius and Stephanus descended the steps together. Neither spoke, but when they reached the little corridor leading to the Emperor's rooms they paused. Silently Parthenius gestured to the wooden box on top of the cupboard. Stephanus found the dagger and hid it in the bandage on his arm. They clasped each other. 'For freedom.' whispered Parthenius.

'For Flavia Domitilla,' answered Stephanus.

Domitian received Stephanus in his bedroom, sitting on his couch. He knew him as Domitilla's freedman. From the folds of his tunic Stephanus produced a sheet of paper. He began to outline the details of a conspiracy which he had uncovered. It involved three senators and the governor of Syria, one Cornelius Nigrinus. A revolt was to be fomented in the east. Stephanus had overheard details being discussed when acting as a butler at a private dinner party in a house on the Esquiline hill. He had a list of the names on the paper in his hand. Might he show it to the Emperor?

As Domitian bent to look at the paper Stephanus drew the dagger from his bandage and thrust it at the Emperor's belly. Domitian sensed the sudden movement. He sprang back with a shriek but the blade cut into his thigh. Screaming, he made a grab at the pillow on his bed in search of his dagger. It was not there; it was in the hand of Stephanus who came at him again. With one hand Domitian held the pillow in front of him while he tried with the other to grab the knife. Blood spurted from his palm as he clutched at the blade. Parthenius moved swiftly to the trapdoor to release

Maximus and Satur who had no weapons. While the Emperor continued to shriek for help they seized his arms. In a frenzy Stephanus brought the dagger down again and again into the Emperor's body until he lay still.

The German bodyguards had heard the shouts. Any injury to the Emperor would mean death in the arena in the jaws of a lion for those who had been on duty. Down the steps they hurled themselves, drawing their swords as they flew along the narrow corridor. At the top of the staircases to the stadium and the terrace, bolts flew back. Shouts for assistance echoed in the high vaults and men began to run hither and thither asking what was happening.

The Germans caught Maximus and Satur as they clambered back into the tunnel under the antechamber. The attendants had no chance and were run through on the spot. Parthenius and Stephanus reached the other end and climbed out into the shrubbery in the stadium. They could hear the guards coming after them in the tunnel. From the porticos more German guards rushed into the garden, screaming vengeance. Above in the gallery stood Norbanus who looked down impassively on the scene below. He was surrounded by a group of praetorians but he gave no orders to them. Stephanus looked up and for a moment their eyes met. Norbanus looked straight through the freedman. Stephanus fought hard but the bodyguards soon had him cornered on one of the little bridges. The spear struck him full in the chest and he fell lifelessly into the canal. Parthenius was taken alive. They stuffed his testicles into his mouth before spilling his guts onto the gravel path. Norbanus turned away and ordered the praetorians to secure the palace. He had an appointment to keep with the new emperor of Rome.

CHAPTER XII

RESURRECTION

When news reached Albanum of the Emperor's death there was great rejoicing among freedmen, slaves and guards alike. The revelry lasted for several days during which Domitian's pleasure boat was taken out onto the lake where it remained anchored during an orgy of feasting and drinking. A few became so drunk that they fell overboard and were drowned. Amongst them was the curator of the menagerie, Massilius, who had climbed onto the rail surrounding the upper deck and attempted to balance there while pouring wine down his throat from a jug. The last that had been seen of him was the soles of his boots as he fell backwards into the night.

Order was restored when the former Empress, Domitia Longina, arrived from Rome. The new Emperor, Cocceius Nerva, had no particular use for Domitian's palace at Albanum and had readily acceded to Domitia's request to be allowed to continue living there. By this time most of the large animals that had previously been kept there had been despatched to the arena in Rome. Nevertheless Domitia, who had a liking for animals generally, decided that she still needed a curator to look after the monkeys, horses, flamingos, swans and other birds which remained. Thus it was that Acilius Bassus, the prefect at Laurentum, summoned Ixus and ordered him to go to Albanum to take charge of the menagerie as an interim measure until somebody permanent was appointed.

Ixus had managed to preserve Raca's cub which was now half grown and lived still in the pen which had been occupied by her mother. Ixus had called the cub Raca too. Each day he had visited the young leopardess, feeding her, talking to her and imitating her sounds. Sometimes, if she was inside the shelter, he would bark softly and Raca would emerge, raise her head to sniff the air and then walk slowly over to where he stood, pressing her flank against the bars so that he could tickle her with his stick.

Ixus went to see his old friend Sergius whom he knew he could trust. Together they loaded the cage containing Raca onto a cart, covering it with a cloth. Round the cage they placed crates of chicken and geese which squawked and cackled loudly throughout the journey, muffling any distressed barking from the leopardess. When they reached Albanum Ixus put Raca into one of the disused pens for a few days, explaining that he had brought the cub from Laurentum to raise by itself as it had a disease which only he could cure.

Ixus's duties were not demanding. The care of the animals at Albanum was easy to organise and he had a team of slaves to carry out the routine feeding and watering. There were no consignments of animals in or shipments out to the arena. Occasionally Domitia came to see her monkeys or perhaps to inspect the giant carp and eels which lived in pools nearby. Ixus took to hunting in the woods where he caught hares and rabbits. Sometimes he shot a deer with his arrows or trapped a wild boar with a spear and a net. One day when he was stalking a deer he almost stumbled over the edge of what turned out to be an old quarry. It had been used many years earlier to provide stone for the foundations of the palace but was now largely overgrown with low scrub which made it difficult to detect. Ixus skirted round the top of the quarry and then walked down the remains of a track which led to the entrance. It did not take him long to realise that the quarry would make a home for Raca. It would be easy enough to fence off the entrance. She would be free to roam in the pit, learning gradually to hunt for herself and live off the rabbits and some of the leaves and berries on the bushes and trees. The quarrying had left several stone ledges and large crevices where the leopardess could bask. At the bottom of the pit a basin of water had formed to provide a drinking pool.

It took Ixus longer than he expected to fence off the entrance to the quarry. There was plenty of timber with which to fashion an effective barrier, but then he found other stretches around the rim where it might be possible for a leopard to climb out and which also had to be fenced. At last, after several weeks of hard work, he was satisfied that the quarry was secure and he brought Raca to it in a horse and cart, up the old track which he had to clear of brambles first. He dragged the carcase of a wild pig into the pit and while Raca crouched to lick the flesh he pushed the mobile cage into some bushes to conceal it before retreating through the palisade with the cart.

For a couple of months Ixus bought meat up to Raca regularly. Occasionally he released into the pit a live pig or deer which he had trapped nearby. He did not always see Raca but he knew that she was catching them, for he found their remains together with the bones of rabbits and the occasional hare. One afternoon he spotted her basking in a tree which grew down by the pool. He sat down on a stone near the water. She stayed in the tree where he could hear her purring. After that Ixus regularly sat on the same stone talking quietly to the leopardess and imitating her soft grunts. Sometimes she would climb down from the tree and settle on her haunches a few yards away from him. He loved the grace with which she moved and the serenity of her face resting on her paws when she lay asleep, her body almost indistinguishable from the surrounding foliage in the dappled light. The pattern of spots on her skin was different from her mother's but to Ixus her face seemed identical. Once he found her swimming in the pool. She heard him coming and he watched as she shook the sparkling droplets from her fur before leaping up into the tree. That evening he left the entrance to the quarry open.

★ ★ ★

On the island of Pandataria Domitilla and her maid Orestilla lived out empty days. The villa in which they lived had been built almost one hundred years before by Julia, the daughter of Augustus, during her period of exile. It had been sumptuously decorated but neglect, the wind and the sea had wrought their work. Domitilla had found a small suite of rooms looking onto the interior courtyard. Here she could sit, sheltered from the wind and the unrelenting sun. There was no escape from the smell of sulphur which pervaded the island. Few plants grew there and no trees could take root in the thin impoverished soil. Everywhere one looked, outcrops of russet coloured tufa sprang raggedly from the ground, the product of the volcano which had thrown up this tiny island in the middle of the Tyrrhenian Sea. In several places green-stained steam hissed gently from the pockmarked rock. Each morning Domitilla walked the circumference of the island, sometimes alone, sometimes with Orestilla if she felt up to it, for her maid was ageing rapidly. They saw no living thing apart from a few lizards which scuttled into the rock crevices at their approach and the ever present gulls whose shrieks and squawks formed an unceasing chorus to the gentle lapping of the sea. In the distance to the east lay another small island and on clear days they glimpsed the coast of Italy and the hazy cone of Vesuvius above the buried town of Herculaneum.

Once a month a supply ship came from the naval base at Misenum bearing meagre supplies of food and fruit. By the end of the month most of the fruit not consumed by the six guards, who had first pick of it, was rotten. As a result the health of both Domitilla and her maid deteriorated. The sun and wind dried their faces which developed the wrinkled appearance of women who worked in the fields.

There was little to do. Domitilla wrote letters which the captain of the guards undertook to have delivered to the mainland, but she had no means of knowing what happened to them once they reached Misenum. No news reached her for she was not allowed to receive correspondence. The guards changed every two months and occasionally she or Orestilla might glean something from an overheard remark. For the most part, however, the soldiers' conversation was mundane and contained nothing of interest. When the supply boat came in, Domitilla was confined to the villa so it was impossible to communicate with the crew. In the evenings she might read so long as the light lasted, but the supply of scrolls was limited and she had soon exhausted them. Orestilla could no longer read to her as she had in the past, for her eyes had faded so that the old freedwoman could not even see to weave.

It became hard to maintain hope. With the passing of the months Domitilla relapsed into periods of speechless inertia.

Her appetite, not helped by the poor quality of the food, diminished. She still made her circuit of the island, early in the morning before the sun had grown too hot. Thereafter listless hours were spent sitting in the shade of the courtyard, half asleep and waiting for another day to end. She began to long for death.

Then one morning when she was stumbling along the shore alone, for Orestilla had grown too weak to accompany her, she was surprised to see a galley pulling into the tiny harbour. The supply ship was not due for some days and she recognised the boat as one of the imperial fleet stationed at Misenum. At the villa she found waiting for her an officer who handed to her a letter from Domitia Longina. The former empress had requested that Domitilla be permitted to return from exile and live with her at Albanum. The officer also brought with him an order sealed by the Emperor Nerva requiring him forthwith to convey the lady Flavia Domitilla to the mainland where she would be carried by coach to Albanum.

★ ★ ★

In the weeks which followed her return Domitilla soon regained her health. The palace on the hill above the lake had acquired a new charm. Gone were the imperial attendants and hangers-on. A light and happy atmosphere prevailed. Domitia maintained a small staff of servants and slaves, for her needs were modest now. There were picnics by the lake and suppers on the terrace. Players came from Rome to perform in the theatre. When her father, the great general Corbulo, had been stationed in the province of Syria Domitia had loved to listen to the tales of another world in the distant east told by merchants who rode on camels over the long trade routes through the mountains and deserts beyond the Caspian Sea, bringing with them silks, ivory, spices and jewels to Parthia and the Roman provinces. She had been very young then but still retained vivid memories of the stories her father had regaled her with before his suicide on Nero's orders.

As soon as she had regained her strength Domitilla took to walking up the hill again. She found the temple and the shrine to Isis, untouched and just how she remembered them. The water still bubbled from the jug into the basin of blue mosaic and the goddess gazed serenely over the lake. Domitilla sat with her memories on the little steps of the temple. Once again she experienced the protective power of Isis who healed her pain and restored her joy. She stroked the ring on her finger. Sometimes she thought she heard his footsteps as twigs snapped under his feet on the path above. One still afternoon, far below in the pasture just above the lake, she watched the figure of a man striding towards the palace from the woods. He was a long way from her so that she could not make out his face. Perhaps she had imagined it, yet the way he moved so easily across the grassy meadow reminded her of Hispo. She watched him intently until his figure disappeared from view.

From time to time Domitia liked to visit her monkeys in the menagerie. Domitilla used to accompany her and together they watched the trainer put the animals through their repertoire of tricks. On one occasion Ixus, who had just returned from the quarry where he had left a stillborn calf for Raca, came past and stopped to watch. Domitilla noticed the young man who seemed very personable. She began to frequent the menagerie more often to watch the animals being fed and exercised. Like others before her, she marvelled at the relationship which Ixus was able to forge with them.

Birds ate from his hand and horses would nuzzle him for no reason. He treated her with great respect, never speaking unless spoken to. Ixus had no idea who Domitilla was but he sensed by the manner of her speech and the quality of her clothes that she was a lady of noble birth. Nevertheless, she seemed friendly and interested in his work. She asked him questions about his earlier life. At first he was reserved but gradually his manner became more open. He started to look forward to her visits. He had never told a single person, other than Sergius who still worked at Laurentum, about Raca. The urge to tell somebody about his leopardess grew until the day he finally revealed to Domitilla that he had another animal to show her.

Domitilla was intrigued. She would love to see the leopardess. 'Where do you keep her? I thought there were no animals of that kind here these days.'

Ixus recounted the whole story of Raca and her mother. He was relieved that he could at last unburden himself to somebody, share his secret and perhaps ensure that the leopardess was allowed to live, if her existence were discovered.

'I cannot be sure that we shall see her. She may have wandered away from the quarry now I have opened the gate,' he explained. 'But there's a good chance. She is still eating food which I leave for her there. We shall have to go at dusk. That's the best time, my lady.'

The following day, when the last rays of the sun were shining horizontally between the trees, and the water of the lake had turned from deep blue to the darkest mauve, Ixus led Domitilla upwards into the woods. The thrushes were calling as they found their last perches for the night and a few deer bounced away through the scrub at their approach. Soon they reached the quarry. Ixus led the way down to the pool and motioned to Domitilla to stop some way before it. She sat down on a slab of rock while Ixus walked a little further forward. In front of him lay the still water with a little beach of shards surrounding three sides of it. Beyond rose a sheer face of rock carved out of the side of the hill. She saw Ixus raise his head and heard him bark softly. No answering sound or movement came. He barked again and then sat down on a rock close to the pool. A bird suddenly squawked and flew up from a tree. Ixus did not move and silence fell again. Domitilla watched intently but could detect nothing. It seemed that Raca was not there. A few minutes passed. Ixus sat stock still and then she saw him slowly turn his head and point towards some bushes a little way above the water. Domitilla strained her eyes. The light had almost gone in the bottom of the pit. She looked again at Ixus and tried to follow where his arm was pointing. Then she saw them: two yellow eyes were staring straight at her from beneath an oak sapling which grew a few yards from the water's edge. She thought she could detect the outline of the leopardess's head. There was no body; it must be directly behind her, hidden in the undergrowth. Domitilla felt herself transfixed by the unblinking stare. She could not tear her own eyes away. She heard Ixus make another sound, more like a grunt than a bark. Suddenly the head rose and a moment later the leopardess was padding silently towards the pool. She crouched and began to lap the water. Domitilla could just make out the sound of purring. At first she thought that it was Ixus, then she realised that Raca was making the noise as she drank. Little ripples ran across the water until eventually the leopardess rose, shook her head and walked slowly back across the shingle to a patch of grass. She sat back on her haunches and then lay down on her stomach, sphinx like with her forepaws out in front. She began to wash.

Ixus sat motionless. Domitilla listened to him talking softly to the leopardess. She had never witnessed such intimacy between a human and an animal. The ghastly cruelty of the amphitheatre and the stench of fear had been her experience. She was astonished at the beauty of this creature who seemed to listen to a young man talking to her in a language she had never heard, a language of understanding to which the leopardess responded in the freedom of nature.

The leopardess rose and glided smoothly into the shadows of the bushes. Ixus walked back towards her. As the young man stood over her Domitilla caught his profile in the pale background of the sky's dying light. In that moment she perceived a truth. She understood that Seth had been defeated; that in the body of Horus, Osiris lived again. Domitilla knew whose son was by her side. She took his hand as he helped her to her feet.